Phoenix MacKenzie
Gravity Wave

"Ah what monsters lurk in the mist of ignorance; to rend flesh from bone and bones to ash, till all that remains is a naked soul, who now knows what lurks within the mist, but will any hear that souls scream?"

Published by Lulu.com

©2011 Lulu

First Lulu printing-June 2011

All rights reserved, which includes the right to reproduce this book or portions there of in and form whatsoever. No portion of this book may be reproduced, stored on and form retrieval system, or transmitted, in any form or by any means, electronic, mechanical, photocopying, recording, or otherwise without written permission of the author.

Distributed by Lulu.com
ISBN-978-1-257-82654-4

To contact the author send your emails to:
phoenix.mackenzie2@facebook.com

Facebook Page: http://www.facebook.com/pages/Author-Phoenix-MacKenzie/195242910515137?ref=hnav

Dedicated to those guiding lights of Heaven,
like stars they show a way:

My Wife Katrina

Rain, Jackie and Angel.

Chapter One: Welcome to the future

Her first breath misted the transparent door of Caron Foster's stasis pod; it had been a cold day in England when she'd stepped into the device. Millions of years may have passed for all she knew, in no more than a blink of an eye. Indeed Caron had inhaled fearfully as the door slid closed and exhaled as a new view met her eyes; a grey haired man wearing what appeared to be a deep blue diving suit. Chills ran down her spine hounded by memories; diving, trapped, fighting for air, cold, bitter dark cold as they died one by one and she… Bright white light, no this was different and he was neither a Prince or a god and this featureless white room was false somehow. Her pounding heart would not relent, palms slapped against the pod's transparent door gesturing that she wanted out; hearing motors straining to slide it open in vain. Mike examined the damaged stasis pod's seal briefly before slamming an elbow against it. Relieved by a hiss of relenting seals, he offered a calming hand to Caron. She gazed around wondering why her eyes should behold a diver, standing in a room so white, so featureless, and just where the heck was this? Were questions that raced through Caron's mind. Yet one question burned deeper than any other, a question on the lips of every human;

"Have they found a cure?" she asked expecting good news.
"I'm sorry to say, but no Miss Foster, now would you…"
"Then why have…?"

"It's complicated Ma'am, how are you feeling" Sergeant Palmer, wafted a hand held bio scanner over Caron as she stood wearing jeans and a green sweatshirt, next to a cylindrical white pod standing like the lower half of a pillar.
"Fine, doesn't feel like I've been in there any time at all." Caron rubbed her arms feeling the chill of a time long passed.
"You haven't, that's the idea, however some of us have grown old and grey." Palmer remarked with a hint of resentment, combing fingers through his silver hair.
"What year is it then?"
"2361 Ma'am."
"Two hundred years, I've been in there TWO HUNDRED YEARS! Caron grasped a chair and sat down before such news knocked her over, "Two hundred," she muttered into hands covering her lightly tanned and rapidly palling face. "I could never fit that many candles on a cake!" She inspected her hands, making sure they hadn't turned into wrinkled skin hanging off bone. "I thought maybe fifty years at the outside but two hundred, I'm a relic, a virtual dinosaur."
"Nothing of the sort, I assure you. Please put this on, you'll soon warm up." Palmer removed a blue vacuum packed uniform from a white chair and sat down, sliding the suit across a simulated marble table top toward her. "Things have reached a crisis point Caron, may I call you Caron?"
"Yes of course, and you?... Your American?"
"Yes Dr Mike Palmer from Arizona, though I haven't been there for over a hundred years, or is it two hundred, time means little anymore." He rubbed a pale white forehead.
"You certainly don't look that old!" Caron began to remove her jeans.
"There have been advances in your absence, those in the scientific community can expect to live two to three hundred years, an advance made through necessity, I am two hundred and thirty five." Mike shifted uncomfortably, standing up "I'll wait outside, just holler when you're done." hatch doors slid open to his approach "Oh you'll need to lose the underwear." Mike felt somewhat hot under the collar as he waited in the corridor outside.

Caron slipped a shapely thirty two year old body into the one piece uniform, made from a thick material giving it a wet suit appearance like those worn by kayakers and surfers. She couldn't help but feel a little aroused by the suit adjusted itself to provide a snug fit; reinforced padding replaced underwear; offering support and a small degree of modesty, although it left little to the imagination. Shoulders, knees, elbows, forearms and spine were also reinforced restricting movement. Caron's heart missed a beat when the suit informed her that 'calibration is complete.' She stood for a moment, wide eyed at private parts of her anatomy being probed, even if for only a gentle moment, she wondered just what the damn thing was 'calibrated' for!

"MIKE!"
"Warming up?" Palmer, still mentally overheated, enquired.
"What does it mean by 'calibration completed', geesh I've tried clothes on, but never had them trying it on with me, not to mention a one liner like calibration completed!" Caron jiggled around as if learning to move again. "And don't for one second even think about telling me we are underwater here… This isn't a diving suit is it?' I won't…."
"No, no we're nowhere near water I assure you. It, err," the suit was doing nothing to keep Mike's mind focused on the job, which certainly wasn't taking mental notes of her every curve and… "Is adjusting to the shape of your body," he swallowed hard "reading your vital signs, temperature, hormones, blood pressure and… so on." Palmer shook his head, rattling a tired and very distracted brain "The arms," he moved a chair next to Caron, sat down and touched her left forearm "will display all sorts of information"
Lights and a visual display appeared between elbow and wrist.
"This will display names of all personnel, should you wish to communicate with individuals. This will communicate with all personnel for general announcements. There is an audio sensor in your collar." Mike gazed up, almost melted by her ruby red lips.
"You will need to spend a few days learning about all this."
"Okay… fine." The thought of that was akin to watching dust form as far as she was concerned. "I look like Batman, well Batwoman I guess." Caron stood up looking down at herself "What about my family, my friends and colleagues, are they all dust now and what the hell happened to my pod!?" Caron noticed that its white

exterior had scorch marks, scratched and dents.

"A lot can happen in two hundred years." Palmer avoided the question "You'll be brought up to date at the briefing. As for your family, I don't know to be honest, perhaps we can look into that later."

"Okay fine." Caron face expressed anything but that. "What does the sand colored band around the arm signify?" She brought her left arm foreword to Mike's attention.

"Uniforms are all the same color, the band indicates rank or profession."

"So your…" Caron adjusted auburn hair to reform an oval framing her face.

"Three gold bands and one silver indicates I'm a Sergeant and scientist, bit of a Jack of all trades and Master of none really; medic, astrophysicist, geneticist, I've had time to learn a bit of this and a bit of that, I was a marine once upon a time."

"So, you're two hundred and thirty five, that's staggering! What about everyone else, you say scientists, what about…."

"They are either dead or in stasis Ma'am" Palmer averted his gaze to the almost featureless table top, then to his hands.

"Dead! What do you mean, the entire human frigging race is DEAD, This isn't real, I'm dreaming this shit!" Caron felt a hypo spray puff against her neck and rapidly felt at ease.

"Calm yourself, no, there are millions of us in stasis, but…" he looked blankly like a man with no hope, drained from decades of trying again and again only to fail again and again "we are running out of time, let alone people Caron, we, scientists have tried to stay alive, tried to fix this mess, but we are dieing, every year there are fewer of us. We bring younger people out of stasis, educating them as our legacy, but its all become pointless anyway. The DNA constantly mutates like its playing with us, laughing at us" Mike fell silent.

"So.. So what am I doing here, where is here, what do you expect an historian to do about any of this, write the human races obituary! Or am I part of a new generation messing around with gook? I'm not cut out for dissecting things and all that."

"Sorry I became self indulgent there for a moment, it's complicated, there is hope, although it feels like we are clutching at straws. Science has done what it can; now it's up to people like

you. No, it's your skills as an archeologist and linguist that maybe required."
"Well spit it out man, and where's the ladies room around here!?"
"You wont need that, just do what you need to do, the suit will take care of it and reduce any waste material to its atomic elements, just as simulators do. There's no need to wash so your quarters, "Mike swept an arm over the room. "has no bathroom, however I think you will feel at home."

After witnessing technology rapidly transform a featureless white room into a simulated version of her old apartment near Oxford University, Caron followed Mike through what was clearly some form of military complex, with it's circular passageways that's metallic uniformity was only broken by entrances to other rooms; sealed shut by reinforced sliding hatches. The cold sterility of it all made her home sick, or at least occupation sick, for she longed to be in some dusty old library or at an archaeological dig availing meaning to ancient languages and symbols.

Caron was an old fashioned girl, technology not being her 'cup of tea.' Indeed she would much rather wait for a kettle to boil than have a simulator present a perfect cup of tea in the blink of an eye. Watching her bed slide out from the wall and make itself, lamps, books and all the other prized junk she adored, revealing themselves from hidden compartments in the floor, ceiling and walls; walls that changed color and pattern in an instant. All this was entertaining to say the least, but a little dust, a coffee stain here and there were lacking and that's what made it home. Even the lack of shadows, lost to the uniform light of luminescent walls, robbed character and gave to conformity. The absence of bathroom facilities disturbed her, though not half as much as being told the suit would take care of bodily functions. 'Oh YUCK' her mind informed as she finally had to go, yet there was no sensation, no walking funny while the suit took care of things. Although the 'viro suit' felt sooo comfortable, Caron walked with arms folded across her chest, not that she was shy, but felt as though she'd been stripped naked and sprayed blue. Her arms relaxed into a normal walking stance at the sight of two other female members of staff who didn't seem concerned about their details being revealed, and a man hadn't given her a second glance. Apparently this was all perfectly normal. Mike, a recent addition to the team, was still trying to get used to it all.

Caron wondered what other surprises the past two hundred years had saved up for her. A deep, distant and rhythmic pounding greeted her ears before they were shielded. She blinked, staring at Mike who now appeared to be wearing some kind of futuristic motorcycle helmet, just like the one she now glared out of.

"Probably an asteroid." Mike shrugged.
"Exactly what year did I loose my sanity?" Caron blinked again.
"Oh it doesn't get any better." Mike touched a red flashing light on her arm display, instantly deactivating her helmet and gloves, which vanished into collar and wrists. "Here we are." he gestured to a hatch marked 'Conference Room.'

Chapter Two: Off to a bad start.

"Please be seated" Captain Lukas Griffin gestured to one of several seats facing a long semi circular desk bristling with displays and controls, arcing around to the left and right of Lukas, who stood on the other side and before a large wall screen which currently displayed the letters: A.R.E.
"Hi" Caron greeted another puzzled individual and sat next to him.
"Jack." He extended a hand.
"Caron Foster, I'm…." She felt the strength of Jack's handshake briefly before Lukas interrupted.
"Caron Foster, Professor of…" Lukas twirled his hands as if trying to generate the right words "Old stuff at Oxford University." He gestured toward her with his left hand "And Lieutenant Jack Dempsey of the now defunct International Intelligence Bureau." Lukas likewise gestured with his right hand.
"Ouu THE Jack Dempsey Mr terrorist hunter!" Caron batted her eyelashes at the famous 38 year old, dark haired cyber hunter, whose strong facial features had dominated the news once upon a time.
"I'm little more than a redundant technician Caron, honestly."
"Hey don't mess with a girls dreams!" Caron gazed into his deep eyes.
"We'll get started, the others are already familiar with our mission and will join us soon, for the moment I think you would both benefit from a brief summery of the last two hundred years since you were last… active, I know I certainly was." Lukas frowned disapprovingly, only adding to his no nonsense appearance.
"What is ARE?" Caron had to stop herself from raising a hand, as her students had so often done in class.
"Astronomical Research and Exploration, which you are now part of, like it or not!" Lukas brought broad shoulders back emphasizing a lean muscular torso, which his suit did little to disguise.
"But…"
"Please, lets allow the presentation to enlighten you first." Griffin stepped to the side making the screen more visible to them. "As you know from our time; the polar shift created havoc with Earth's

weather systems." He scrolled through several images of floods, landslides, forest fires and frozen cities "To make matters worse the tectonic stress of this shift led to ever increasing volcanic action." More visions of an emerging hell met their eyes; blackened sky, towns and cities shattered, refugee camps that had once only been associated with third world countries were now common in the West. "San Francisco… gone, Rome finally devoured in a second earthquake, the damn place just swallowed by Earth's fury. To make matters worse," the upper floors of skyscrapers featured in series of images "London, Berlin, Moscow, Paris are under that snow and ice somewhere."

"An ice age, it's…" Jack slowly shook his head.

"Mass exodus, but there was nowhere to run, every nation had its catastrophes, the economic consequences made it increasingly difficult to help anyone, civilization broke down." Images of people starving in refugee camps, riots, tanks and suppression by military forces appeared and faded, offering a horrific story of suffering and civilizations falling.

"Oh my GOD!" Caron's jaw dropped.

"Yes, sorry that was after your time Caron, the freeze spread rapidly a few years after your stasis."

"As if sterility wasn't enough!" A tone of anger resonated in Jack's voice.

"Mars station became a refuge, the main source of energy to sustain stasis units, that's where you have spent the past one hundred and eighty five years. However, many millions… Billions did not survive the devastating affects of this shift. Plans to place half the world population in stasis were just not feasible. As if nature wasn't enough we ended up killing each other in civil wars…. Perhaps better than starvation for many. " Lukas stared at the floor deep in depressive thought.

"Why was I transported to Mars? What happened to the stasis centre in Washington… or shouldn't I ask?"

"Jack there is no Washington, there is no America. The super volcano in Yellowstone Park blew filling the sky with ash for many years, shrouding the northern hemisphere in darkness. We're not sure if it was that or the shift that led to the ice age in the Americas."

"Did anyone survive, apart from us I mean, I mean are we IT?"

Caron's eyes streamed tears, but emotions were soon calmed. Her hand darting up to her neck, reacting to a hypo spray puffing a host of hormone stabilizing enzymes. She frowned, uncomfortable with feelings being manipulated. Surely any human being should be horrified by such news. Now Caron felt as if the news were fiction or like so many events she'd studied in history that had long passed; detached from it, the world had moved on, civilizations rebuilt, yet now… She pondered, yes now was a time for keeping a cool head if humanity was ever to rebuild.

"Earth is abandoned, well apart from a dozen stasis centers that survived the catastrophes, a few research stations are still operating. Our dilemma there is that power stations are becoming unstable, droids maintain them, but when the power goes down they have a limited time to fix things before their cells are drained. We don't have the human resources to rebuild or create new stations."
"What about the colonies?" Jack asked, searching for some hope.
"The colonies, well Africia, Centauri Five and Ashari are fine, though of course everyone is in Stasis. Technology has been refined on those worlds that haven't endured natures more violent means of revenge."
"That's something at least, but still no cure, what hope ultimately is there?" Jack's arms swung out to the sides, his body language expressing 'where'.
"No, our scientists have worked tirelessly for centuries, women still can't conceive, the great mother of them all seems to be saying your time is over. We've had some success, a few children have been born in 2291, 2315, twins Dharma and Arten in 2337. However the genetics governing reproduction mutated again and again."
"We are in little doubt that there is an intelligence behind this." Mike added, "Like a programmed response to our own genetic manipulation."
"Artificial bodies were created, usually resulting in the simplification of the poor souls that tried it, others just destroyed themselves." Lukas displayed a few pictures of virtual manikins crouched in corners of rooms.

"Okay, okay, I've heard enough, I just, I mean what's the friggin point, did you just wake us up to torture us with this, this shit?" Caron tried to express a modicum of anger and relieved that no puff prevented at least that feeling.

"There is… Hope." Lukas looked away from them as if doubting his own words and concerned as to how they might react to such vain hope, he certainly hadn't liked the taste of it when presented to him. "You Miss Foster may play a central role in a mission that is, to be frank; a long shot, however, what have we to loose!"

"Oh, I get to be a super hero at last! Do I get any special powers? Like erm… maybe…" She wiped away previous tears "Guess, this suit thing doesn't wash your face for you, anyone got a tissue?" She sniffed "Oh GEE thanks" Caron mumbled inside her helmet.

"No problem." Jack pressed an indentation on her left forearm again, retracting the helmet to reveal a refreshed face.

"What happens if I sneeze? NO, no it's okay, I'll save that for later!" she raised hands as if to guard herself.

"No superheroes I'm afraid, though we do have… Anyway, your knowledge of linguistics, mythology, archaeology and, and well I guess that's it, is why your needed here." Lukas explained.

"Here? Where is here?" Caron mimicked Jack's previous body language.

"Oh, somewhere between Sirius and Alpha Centauri." Lukas brought up an image of stars. "SERGEANT," he yelled at Mike who sat humming a tune "could you possibly remain in the land of the here and now long enough to escort our other guests here?"

"Yes Sir" Mike eased himself up and left the room.

"We're on a space ship?" Caron eyes widened nervously.

"It's a three year journey to Alpha Centauri alone, how long's it gonna take to get to Sirius, five hundred years?" Jack scuffed.

"Takes two weeks for Alpha Centauri now, this old bucket has been refitted with some … well don't quite understand what it is myself yet, but its some kinda device that manipulates gravity into a stream, like riding a wave that flows from one sun to another."

"Old bucket?" Jack seemed doubtful, all this was from the future as far as he was concerned.

"Unbeknown to many, the US government had been constructing a small fleet of military space craft, you are aboard the Argo, an Eagle class carrier, somewhat like a small aircraft carrier."

"Oh what just in case the mighty pirate fleet attacks with their secret death ray? Oh wait no was it to prevent aliens from landing and turning us all into chicken soup? More like they had too much money and needed to throw it away on some insane project!" Jack expressed usual political frustrations.

"Well, other than pirate hunting, this vessel is finally fulfilling its intended purpose in a round about way." Lukas swept a palm over his shaven head.

"You mean there are aliens!?" Caron looked from Lukas to Jack and back again, as if looking for some reassurance that she wasn't going insane.

"There were aliens, whether there still are remains to be seen, we are talking about millions of years ago though and some very old ruins are all we have as evidence."

"OOHHHHH, something finally makes sense" Caron squirmed and smiled in a way that if anyone had doubts about her sanity they would now be confirmed. "Do I get to dig around in the dirt then?"

"Yes you get to dig around in the dirt, firstly I would like you to examine these images of ruins and artifacts from Mars."

"MARS! What the hell?" Caron strided to the screen to get a closer look at the third dimension image of a monoliths glyphs projecting out from the screen a few inches..

"These relics have been known about since the early landings in the twenty first century, it was thought best to keep such matters quite however, don't want to upset the peasants you know. Some of the glyphs have been interpreted, but I'm sure you will want to form your own opinion. They have set our present course however."

"What else is on Mars?" Caron glared at Lukas as if he'd committed a grievous crime.

"A great deal, it's actually where we attained stasis technology, artificial gravity and French fries." The Captain's attempt at humor was lost to Caron's intense focus on the glyphs. "But of course you would be more interested in the monuments and pyramids and such, all in good time."

"The glyphs are not dissimilar to some of those found in underwater cities," Caron mumbled to herself.

"Is this old bucket going to get us there in one piece, sounded like we hit something back there?" Jack's time onboard a space station had not been without incident.

"She's armed to the teeth, those were pulse cannons you heard removing obstacles in our path, the hull is constructed of an alloy that can take direct hits from sizable asteroids, another gift from our alien friends. Your suits are multi environment, they can protect you from extreme temperatures and so forth, you can learn more about them later."

"Another gift from the aliens?" Caron looked down dubiously at her firmly supported breasts.

"No, there have been numerous by-products from our research into genetics and artificial life forms over the years."

"You're telling me there's an artificial life form sticking its whatever in my whathaveyou!?" Caron's eyes darted toward her butt.

"Not quite, the suit doesn't have it's own consciousness, though it is artificially intelligent, it tries to anticipate to some degree."

"So what did you get me out of bed for?" Jack put his feet up on a chair. "My skills were obsolete long ago and my knowledge of DNA is somewhat out of date."

"It's your ability to analyze, detect and modify we require Jack, the skill pool of those that have worked in our absence has its limits, you may have to tinker with things to suit your needs."

"The aliens left some DNA for us then?"

"No, solar radiation removed all traces of life from Mars, but we have samples from Earth that we want both of you to work with, and it's the donor of that DNA we are attempting to find. Difficult as circumstances have taken their toll, even the more recent samples we have are incomplete, but enough to match others throughout the ages."

"Not making a whole lot of sense Captain," Jack tensed with frustration.

"Then I'll explain our mission, which to be honest… Well form your own opinions; we are searching for a god!"

"Yep when all else fails we can always pray I guess," Caron's attention was diverted from the subject, which had bounced from utter despair to hopeless to interesting and now ridiculous. By the swish of automatic doors opening behind her, "Ohhhhh my God!" her jaw dropped and tears began to well up again, "So beautiful," thoughts escaped her lips as the sight that beheld her mesmerized.

"It's true then," Jack, likewise stunned, gazed as the twins took their seats with a graceful smile in return for amazement, "second generation Ashari?"

The word 'greetings' and a sense of love filled minds as the Ashari nodded in Caron and Jack's direction. Few people from Earth had ever visited Ashari, other than the psychic colonists who had little choice other than to settle there, as their abilities had become socially unacceptable on Earth. People disliked not being able to keep thoughts to themselves, feeling inadequate when others could levitate or move objects through powers of mind and energies beyond comprehension of sciences limited attitudes. Humanity no longer felt safe with such powers at the disposal of a few and so those with such abilities welcomed an opportunity to create their own civilization, which thrived. Yet it did not escape the genetic time bomb resulting in women's ovaries no longer producing eggs. Other than a few temporary successes no human child had been born for two hundred and ten years. Many people had been placed in stasis until a cure could be found, they remained, still waiting for that miracle.

The twins were amongst the first children to be born as true Ashari natives. With their second generation parents also born on Ashari, the twins had no direct connection to Earth and it showed. A combination of Ashari's atmosphere and its red dwarf sun, affected those born there in striking ways. Jack and Caron were understandably mesmerized by sapphire blue eyes, white hair complimenting skin with a violet pigment rather than human pink, their blood being purple rather than red. Slightly lower gravity on Ashari also resulted in a petite bone structure giving them almost elfin features. Far from being frail and weak, minerals and nutrients from Ashari's soil and vegetation resulted in extremely high density, diamond like bones and teeth. Within just a few generations Ashari's became cousins of the human race; rare, mythical, refined and powerful.

"Actually third generation, Dharma and Arten are one of the rare successes with our DNA manipulation, it was thought we might have more luck with Ashari's given their, erm… altered state, but alas we faired no better with them. Arten and Dharma," Lukas gave the twins a wave, "are adding their remarkable talents to our team. However, guys I would appreciate it if you could communicate as we do, humans are not comfortable with anyone else in our heads okay?"

"Apologies, we will try." Arten nodded.

"Beautiful." Caron repeated still in a daze.

"Thank you." Arten and his Sister smiled shyly, unaccustomed to socializing.

"Sooo what can you angels do then?" Jack's frustration turned to apprehension, something Dharma and Arten were acutely aware of, their gaze turning to one another.

"We use psychometry to touch the past and we feel many other things, from people and objects." Dharma turned to Arten.

"We can also touch others with feelings and memories…"

"Nightmare those two when they were kids, first time Arten had a tantrum he fried everything electrical at the research centre, no sooner did we get around that one when they started throwing things at us with their devious little minds…., HEY quit that" Mike started to float as Dharma giggled.

"Okay, okay behave! The rest of our crew you'll meet in the coming weeks, Jack here helped to develop the DNA tracking system which virtually eliminated crime and put himself out of a job in the process. Some of us, such as engineers, technicians and flight crew were brought out of stasis a year or two ago, we also have thirty marines. This is essentially a science vessel now, but it's better to be prepared for any eventuality." Lukas stepped to the side again, displaying another Image and pausing for a reaction.

"Thoth?" Caron questioned the reason for the image rather than any doubt as to who it was.

"Yes, we are looking for Thoth; at least the evidence leads us to suspect this is the case, Thoth being one of many aliases. Scientists attempting to discover some answers from our genetic history came upon an enigma as they examined what museums had to offer. Two relics from different parts of the world had traces of the same genetic fingerprint. An Egyptian dagger dated 1035 BC and the quill from the British royal household dated 1573 AD. So, using your DNA tracking system we detected the same ID again and again throughout history." Lukas displayed a repeated image of a DNA helix.

"Taking samples from relics that old hardly provides concrete evidence, the DNA could," Jack brought up the image on a desk screen zooming in, highlighting various strands and sequences "obviously corrupted, could be plant or animal…" something triggered confusion in his mind, urging him to select another sample "it's the same, the same coding… but this isn't human coding, well not entirely anyway."

"Nope." Lukas crossed arms, resting his back against a wall waiting for Jack to acknowledge many years of research, checking, cross checking.

"Alien?" Caron peered over Jack's shoulder.

"Can't be anything else, these base pairs are unidentified, no match to anything known on the atomic chart, no match to any living thing on Earth, yet the basic structure is the same as human DNA, double helix, all this, this and this pretty standard stuff, but here" he pointed to strands with bases colored grey "here and there for example, that isn't human. Any theories on what boss?" Jack glanced toward Lukas.

"Nope, don't look at me; I have no idea what you're talking about!"

"Well DNA looks like a ladder when you untwist it; base pairs are the rungs of the ladder."

"Okay, with you so far."

"Each rung has two parts, one is screwed into the left strand and one into the right strand so to speak, we call them bases. There are four different types of bases, like four different jigsaw puzzle pieces, now piece one and two will fit together and make a pair; a rung. Piece three and four fit together and make a pair, but piece four and one won't fit together, so they wouldn't make a rung."

"So how does that affect the price of rice?" Caron squinted at a ladder with colored rungs marked A,T,C and G.

"It's like Morse code, dots and dashes, this pair make a dot, this pair make a dash, a sequence of dots and dashes make a word. This is just like that code; pairs in a sequence make up a code that produces proteins, which, to cut a long story short, are what makes you, your charming self."

"Flattery will get you everywhere." Caron playfully flirted, though her attention remained with the DNA strand, "Looks like your ladder is broken Jack."

"As I say you can't expect samples that are thousands of years old to be perfect, have a look at our quill sample." Jack scrolled to the next image, then the next and the next and back again. "This is the same sample," he looked accusingly at Lukas as if annoyed by such a simplistic data error.

"No, they are as indicated, different samples, from different times and places." Mike remarked.

"All broken rungs, I mean pairs, the same pairs are missing again and again, you're kidding me right?"

"Nope."

"Wouldn't fancy climbing that ladder." Caron sat down again.

"I wouldn't fancy meeting the glob of jelly this DNA belongs to!" Jack sat back hard in his seat.

"We reached the conclusion that this fingerprint has been planted. It gives us evidence that it's not human, or not entirely human and that it's been messed with. We can connect it to this Thoth character with some degree of certainty but other samples sources are contaminated with human DNA traces." Sergeant Palmer sat next to Caron, feeling included in this new team.

"Catch me if you can!" Caron suggested.

"Exactly." Mike confirmed.

"That's the game we are playing now people, although we can only guess at what we're looking for, we at least have a partial genetic fingerprint."

"Why would Thoth leave an intentional trail?" Caron shrugged.

"It is… intentional and yet not." Arten cryptically shared his feelings.

"It is natural though." Dharma added.

"What do you mean" Jack voiced a question shared by others.

"What is missing has died or…" Arten struggled with words.

"Been reclaimed." Dharma attempted to clarify with little success

"May we share?" she turned to Lukas.

"Very well." Lukas approved with a degree of apprehension.

A vision of DNA nucleotides breaking free and drifting toward a human shaped radiant white light filled the minds of the entire crew. It all had a sense of the divine, as if a god were summoning planets and stars to become part of itself again. The feeling overwhelmed crew members who stopped their tasks, stood in a stupor along corridors and lost their train of thought. Lukas was quick to broadcast a ship wide announcement to ignore what just happened and mentally kicked himself for not pre-empting the telepathic influence.

"Could you try to be more selective… or something in future Guys?"
"We will try," Dharma's eyes rolled to heaven.
"It is beyond our ability at the moment Mr. Lukas, we can focus on one person or many, but not a selected few," Arten explained.
"Erm… that was… hmm. So your saying the donor of this DNA took it back, kinda vacuumed himself together again?"
"We can only offer what we feel Mr. Jack," Arten shrugged.
"That makes sense in a sort of can't possibly make sense way!" Caron smiled, becoming more convinced she was dreaming, so what the heck go along for the ride and maybe Spiderman would make an appearance. "Ummm, so where does Spiderman… erm Thoth come into all this?"
"Spiderman!?" Jack laughed.
"Yes well… He's kinda hot; leaping into people's rooms and ties them up…. And things." Caron gazed dreamily, 'things' had been absent from her life for too long, even before stasis.
"NO" Dharma and Arten shook their heads in response to Lukas glaring at them.
"Anyway, new relics were found," a stream of treasures and various items, many ancient, made brief appearances on the screen "including one that the Catholics had been hiding away in the new Vatican; The Hand of Thoth."
"A hand?" Caron was intrigued.
"No, it's a clay imprint, as you can see it's simply a block of clay with a hand imprint, we gather one of a pair that formed a mould, the other would obviously have details of the hand's palm…."
"Ahhh, are we back to rungs again? Like with the… Okay I'll just shut up now." Caron responded to various 'what planet are you on' facial expressions.
"Within the clay of this upper mould a few hairs were preserved. The mould was used several times and we gather that in a later usage it matches the hand of this guy." Lukas presented an image

of a life sized golden Thoth statue. "Claimed from ruins of the old Vatican, they obviously couldn't move such an object without attracting a great deal of attention, But of course you are aware of that Caron."
"Yes, how history changed within a few months of that earthquake!" she almost growled "Sooo, you're sure they are a match?"

Caron wasn't prone to taking peoples word for such matters. So much of Earth's history had been fictitious; written with bias and old school ideas of how things should have been in a very black and white world of academic ego. Her philosophy was that beliefs and theories should never be referred to as fact and that history is the property of all, not a select few, who have something to hide.

"Fits like a glove."
"Okay so how did some dude walk through history looking like a damn bird without turning any heads, other than Egyptian ones, that is?" Jack crossed his arms "It makes no sense."
"Poetic license of the times?" Caron shrugged "The ancient Egyptians were fond of their symbols and symbology, Gods represented aspects of life, of nature, Thoth was associated with knowledge, the bringer of written language, the voice of RA, so you might say he was a divine channel of celestial knowledge… might fit the bill of an alien."
"True but it's his 'bill' that's the problem!"
"He was also depicted as a Baboon Jack, as I say it's all symbolic, it's the meaning of that symbology, his attributes that matter. It's said that he was self begotten, self produced, what did we just see thanks to our remarkable friends here; DNA returning to its source! He was the master of both physical and divine law."
"That's all so much myth and mystical bull though" Mike huffed.
"Science can be blind Mike, you can't find the answers to humanities dilemma and now we are looking for a god! I'm no proponent of religion, but there is middle ground, we need to go way back and embrace the parents of science." Caron rebuffed.
"What light some incense and chant or something?"
"Ha scientists! Whether you want to admit it or not mysticism gave birth to modern science and there is truth in mythology if you

know how to read it. Myths tell more than a story, look at the legend of the Phoenix, what it really relates to is alchemy and transformation of consciousness, the gathering of elements and so on. Alchemy became chemistry; the combining of elements. We just use a different language these days and as you know the ancients weren't a bunch of cave dwelling idiots, well not all of them anyway. You know what I tell my students; don't believe a damn word I say, investigate, prove it to yourself, don't be like sheep mindlessly believing everything you're told."

"Okay I submit." Mike was too fatigued to continue an old argument that had been lost by academics before his time.

"He's credited with making calculations for placement of the heavens, the Earth and stars which may mean he had navigational knowledge, though I doubt Thoth would have revealed much and even then misled to some degree, just as we have seen with his DNA. He governed science, religion, philosophy magic and mathematics, although all of them may have seemed like magic to those who he taught."

"So you believe it's possible then, this guy was Thoth?" Jack hoped for logical conclusions.

"I guess, I mean it's not so fanciful when you bring it down to Earth, if you'll excuse the pun. However, that still casts no light on his presence thousands of years later, unless he can actually reform himself… or something?" Caron glanced over at Arten and Dharma who sat quietly serene together.

"I have to admit, seeing these two grow up makes me feel anything is possible." Mike raised an eyebrow. "However, it was environmental factors that changed these guys and we are dealing with Earth in Thoth's case. Although I certainly don't believe Mr Thoth is a native of Earth."

"Perhaps none of us were." Lukas suggested "Once upon a time. I mean after what I've seen of Mars, you know the layout of the pyramids in one area bares a striking resemblance to those in Cairo."

"Considering the name of that city in ancient times means Mars, it doesn't surprise me." Caron added.

"Are we coming from the angle that Thoth caused the DNA crisis or that he might have an answer to it?" Jack questioned Lukas.

"That we are not judging at the moment, but certainly we hope he has an answer. The last trace of his DNA was dated at 2012, either he didn't reform or left; avoiding the crisis."

"Where did you find the last trace?" Jack scrolled through DNA samples.

"Africia on fragments of a crystal. However the crystal originated on Earth, transported to Africia by one of the settlers. The crystal had been mounted in a silver clasp, part of a pendant, the DNA survived any cleaning within the clasp, its fortunate she didn't discard the broken keepsake." Mike leant over to Jack's console, finding the sample with a few touches of its display.

"Recycling would certainly take care of that evidence, though I have to say it's beyond remarkable that many of these samples were attainable at all, which I guess just adds weight to the planting evidence theory. Can we be sure this isn't a fraud?" Jack pondered.

"That would require planting evidence in a temple chamber which hasn't been opened in three thousand years, until we detected our DNA fingerprint under the city of Cairo." Mike gestured for Lukas to show the image of what they found. "A chamber which contained the usual Egyptian dedications to gods and goddesses; Isis and Osiris if I remember correctly and some politician or other. What's interesting is the focus of astronomy…"

"Sirius?" Caron hardly had to ask "Sirius was important to the Ancient Egyptians, so someone must have inspired them, revealed something of its importance."

"I guess we'll find out soon enough." Lukas gestured to the door, let's get some chow and then give you a tour. I imagine you'll be eager to familiarize yourself with the lab we have set up for… geesshh!" Lukas joined others as they grasped desks or fell to the floor "What the hells going on? Report!" he yelled as the ship juddered and gravitational forces rolled Caron against a wall.

Chapter Three: In the event of an emergency....

"Unknown, sensors inoperable, poss... feedback... Sirius mag... magnetic storm" a broken reply came from Argo's Bridge "Light speed exceeding ninety..."
"Get us out of here, shut down the wave." Lukas barked.
"D, d, dangerous, could..."
"AHHHH" Jack's grasp slipped resulting in his body hurling over the desk and sliding along a vibrating floor.
"We must stop meeting like this!" Caron protested, looking down at Jack's helmet firmly planted in her chest, their bodies mangled together "I can't move, what....?"
"Activating emergency protocol, in five seconds, four seconds, three..." Shom; Argo's automated seductive female voice informed crew.
"Cancel protocol." Lukas wasn't desperate enough to allow a computer to take full control of Argo.
"Emergency protocol cancelled Captain."
"What's going on!?" Jack tried to move, but still sandwiched Caron between himself and a wall.
"I'm not sure... Kern activate Titan level four." Lukas slowly stood up walking toward the hatch in jerky robotic movements.
"Immense gravity, those suits are all that's stopping you from being crushed."
"Yeti activate Titan level four." Mike emerged from behind the desk peering over at tangled crew members "Okay guys be right with you." He crawled toward Caron and Jack, reaching for controls near their wrists.
"Oh geesshh." Jack finally pushed himself away from the wall with the aid of his suit's hydraulic Titan mode; designed for use in high gravity environments.
"There," Mike activated Caron's suit "you'll need to name your suit to use voice commands if you ever..."
"Shom open conference room hatch." Lukas stabbed a control panel with an armored finger, which only resulted in strained tones from door motors.
"Unable to complete command, stress factors are exceeding..."

"Dammit." Lukas tried to force doors apart, their smooth surface giving nothing to grasp. "Bridge report."
"Extreme turbulence…" Lieutenant Yoto's shaky voice only emphasized the obvious.
"No shit! Cause?"
"Exceeding ninety light Sir, anti grav quit at sixty, I don't… analyzing." Yoto tried to make sense of readings that didn't.
"It is the diamond star Mr Lukas." Dharma wasn't sure if she should interrupt amidst the turmoil.
"Sirius B? Uuhhgg"

Lukas flew across the room landing on his knees against a wall, which now served as a floor, then ceiling. Crew tumbled out of control as the Argo mimicked a ship caught in a storm at sea, pounded by unknown forces. Sparks flashed on the Bridge as crew smashed into consoles, suits that protected them were demolishing systems and anything else they hit. The fact that suits were in Titan mode didn't help either as crew tried to grab anything they could while thrown around, resulting in chairs being ripped from floors. Ensign Kartha screamed, flying toward 3D screens displaying stars, easily perceived as windows in the panic and confusion of the moment. Her impact dismissed stars leaving a bare wall. Other panels soon blinked out leaving the Bridge with no view other than that of equipment shattering amidst sparks and human cannon balls.

"Shom, execute emergency PROOOtocol NOW" Lukas yelled between impacts, surrendering human control of a ship was not his way, but circumstances left no choice.
"Emergency protocol activated.. Analyzing… insufficient data, sensor feed damaged, attempting to stabilize…" Shom gave a running commentary of her actions, seemingly detached, cold and logical to all, yet she wasn't simply a bunch of circuits, chips and programming, she felt blind angst.
"Oh mercy it's the floor" Caron lay spread eagled while the Argo tilted and rumbled.
"I want off at the next stop!" Jack got to his knees, grasping the desk.
"Everyone okay?" Lukas checked one of two consoles still in one

piece.

"Yeah think so." Mike looked around, helping Dharma to her feet.

"Yoto… Yoto report." The Captain waved for everyone to sit down as Shom struggled to maintain stability.

"Carnage here Captain, the Bridge is heavily damaged, I'm trying to get things put together, should be able to restore basic controls in an hour."

"Anyone hurt?"

"No, no we're fine." Yoto replied hesitantly, feeling like his brain had been scrambled.

"Dammit" Lukas slammed hands on the desk "I can't get anything out of this." he glared at a console.

"Looks okay." Mike peered over the Captain's shoulder.

"Yeah this is fine, ship's sensors are damaged, I can't get readings on the energy stream, life support, the freakin lunch menu, nothing!"

"I don't think this consol has command clearance for the lunch menu." Mike laughed.

"Of course, Shom give me helm control at this station."

Lukas cursed his lack of experience with this class of ship. Other than recent training flights on the Argo, his last flight had been as Captain of colonial vessels transporting settlers to Alpha Centauri, more of a caretaker role than anything else. It was his former role in exploration that earned him the honor of commanding this mission. Keeping a cool head in a crisis deemed more important than technical experience, exploration, back in the day, was a very dangerous endeavor. Corporations cut corners and it was they that funded military forces in the twenty second century. Lukas had also earned a reputation as a pirate hunter, both on the high seas and space as civilizations began to fall.

"That's more like it, still nothing from sensors though, we are flying blind."

"It is the diamond star Sir." Dharma timidly repeated.

"Oh yes you said, tell me what you see." Although Lukas was greatly concerned by ominous sounds of a creaking, groaning hull, he could not ignore the twins potential to assist when unknown influences endangered the mission, not to mention lives.

"It is like a," she closed eyes "a river of light flowing from the little diamond and another river from the big star and they…"
"Like a Y." Arten added.
"Yes, sort of, like that." Dharma brought her wrists together splaying hands, gesturing a Y shape.
"I think that's possibly the solar energy streams they are seeing." Mike suggested "We should be riding the Sirius A stream, but if its sister star's orbit is on our side of Sirius A, then Sirius B's stream may intersect, though I would have thought it unlikely, B has an orbit of fifty years… although… hmmm."

While attempting to mentally calculate orbits, in relation to their approach from Alpha Centauri, Mike visualized the Sirius system with its two stars, the smaller white dwarf, no larger than Earth, orbiting the massive white star; sizing it up like a gladiator. Oddly the mightiest of these gladiators being the smallest known as Sirius B with a surface density three hundred times that of diamond and core density ten times that staggering armor. B span on its axis not once every twenty four hours like Earth, but twenty three times a minute generating immense magnetic storms; ripping matter from its larger sister Sirius A. Once every fifty years a titanic battle for supremacy in the heavens took place as the gladiators tumbled over each other. Hairs stood up on Mike's neck, if they were being pulled by those forces there was no hope. Far from being in the Heaven's, this was Hell.

"I don't know Captain, I wouldn't have though that a magnetic storm could affect us, we are too far out, if those storms had that much power there would be no planets in the Sirius system, they'd have been ground to dust long ago, but I'm an amateur at astrophysics." Mike shrugged, "Could cause feedback on the star streams though."
"Yeah and the cow jumped over the moon." Jack suggested, having very little idea of what Mike was talking about.
"With aid from a gravity wave this ship generates we are riding, surfing energy which streams between stars its…" Lukas struggled for simple terms "An electrical current, it has polarities like a magnet and creates gravitational…"
"Yeah, I'm with ya, so we are like a kayak on white water hurling

through rapids at Shit Creak and whoops we lost the damn paddle?"

"You could put it that way yes, although we still have a paddle… just about." Lukas's attention returned to the console's display, trying to make sense of the few readings it offered. "Mike see if you can locate Yakov and get some answers about the star's orbit."

"No communication with the lower decks Captain, and he's not in his quarters, last known location…" Mike's sheathed fingers darted over icons on a display screen finding out what he could about the resident astrophysicist "hanger deck, shuttle craft two, calibrating atmospheric…"

"I think we should shut the drive down until…" Lukas grasped the desk as Shom dealt with more turbulence. "What the hell was that?" he responded to a loud creak resonating through the hull.

"Hull breach imminent, hanger bay doors buckling." Shom replied.

"If that goes the whole damn thing goes!" Lukas brought up gravity wave controls on the adjacent console, his mind perceiving both time and options slipping through fingers like sand.

"Wait, if," Jack wasn't sure of himself, but his guts told him to speak up "if you shut down that drive we have no paddle right?"

"It's not that simple Jack," Lukas had no time or inclination for explanations.

"I'm sure, but when kayaking you never stop paddling in white water, you have to read the river and choose your path with it or the river will take you down."

"At the moment we can't see the river, sensors are down so we can't do anything but get off the damn white water." Mike commented.

"Your both right we need an exit but without careful navigation we could end up…" Lukas's heart raced as the ship shuddered again, he knew they had to do something fast but the options were to die one way or another.

"If there's a fork in the river it gets rough, currents here and there, so you go for the strongest current rather than fighting it… and just hope there's not a drop, or a stopper or a…" Jack tried to persuade, having no desire to drown in space; been there, almost done that.

"Dharma what did you see, was there a stronger force, you know one light or stream stronger than another?" The Captain's hand hovered near gravity wave controls.

"The diamond felt stronger, its flow had rage."
"Show me, just me could you?"

Dharma shared her vision of two stars, one large, another tiny sparkling crystalline, energy flowing from them toward Argo. Indeed Lukas saw rivers, yet the water of these were multi colored electrical waves and currents. Sensors enabled them to see these streams, but not in such vivid detail. He could feel the power and chaos overwhelming him.

"Okay, okay, thank you Dharma" Lukas shook his head "I can't tell what's what from that, I see what you mean though."
"It is something you must feel with your whole self." Arten advised.
"Yah, I, maybe with practice," Lukas fought for a polite response as there imminent doom crept ever closer and Argo empathically trembled. "Yoto, any progress?"
"Nothing significant Sir." Yoto looked up from a mass of technology he was trying to salvage without the assistance of engineers.
"Critical failure in generators three and four divert…iiiiinnng" Shom's voice slowed as if someone had just pressed her off button, "power from all non essential systems." Argo plunged into darkness.

Her tone returned to normal, now powered by one of two remaining generators that didn't serve engines, life support and the gravity wave. Emergency lighting illuminated areas of the ship where crew were detected, though now only a thin band of horizontal white light shoulder high provided just enough to see by. A Panel dropped open revealing oxygen generators and portable Compressed Air Propulsion packs capable of propelling an adult sixty five MPH in Earth gravity and a great deal faster in low gravity environments. Mike grabbed the first one handing it to Lukas. He turned expecting another to slide down.

"Damn things jammed up the feeder shaft I think," Mike peered up behind wall panels "Yeti, night vision." The atomic structure of a formerly translucent visor transformed his helmet to a solid,

seemingly visorless blue. "Yah these rods are bent." Grasping two steel rods Mike gave his suit another command "Yeti, Titan ten."
"MIKE!" Lukas yelled to no avail.

Steel rods twisted like putty before snapping, wrenched out of the cavity taking wall panels with them, falling onto and around Mike along with ten CAP packs. Several light sections blinked out in the process sending the Conference Room into even dimmer light levels. Mike handed out the rectangular packs that most outdoor adventurous types were familiar with. Caron bit her lip, enzymes puffed into her neck attempting to counteract the influence of memories. This was getting all too familiar to her. The twins had already been trained to use this equipment and helped each other buckle up. With faces now hidden behind dark helmet visors they chose to see a digital version of the room, overcoming the difficulties of low light. Digital being one of various options such as infrared, ultra violet, even virtual, which could make others appear as monsters, fairies and such in role playing games. Jack and Caron hadn't yet been taken through basic training, whilst Jack was familiar with civilian versions of all this, Caron's dislike of technology didn't prepare her for anything other than a torch. In her mind the dark room was filling with water, just like the mini sub she'd been trapped in, she was only one of three that survived from a crew of seven on a high tech deep sea mission.

"NOOOOO" Caron screamed, throwing Jack across the room "I can't breath, I can't see." she clawed at the dark visor. "Get me out of here." Caron wept, her arms thrashing around trying to find something to grasp, ice cold water lapping around her waist in the dark abyss as the submarine hit bottom.
"It's okay, its okay, just breathe, deep breaths." Jack peeled himself off a wall and held her.
"Sssso sooo cold."

Caron shivered living another time, almost another life and no puff of enzymes could convince her otherwise. She wrapped her arms around Jack as she had around Duncan all those years ago as they shivered together at the bottom of an ocean. It was the cold that took him, others drowned. 'Just breath' he'd said as air thinned.

There was a light now, this was it, no not a tunnel, an angel that was it, sooo beautiful, so peaceful now. Her body fell limp.

"Miss Caron, its okay." Arten wadded through waters of her mind "You're safe now, it's okay." He wasn't so sure about that, but Arten could at least try to assist in one crisis at a time.
"ALERT, HULL BREACH ON DECK ONE, SEALING HATCHES ONE D, ONE N, ONE M, ONE S, ONE T…"
"Shit we've got people down there, Yakov, Rhianna, Zack, ZACK." Lukas yelled at the consol, it's light reflecting from his dark visor, static being the only reply.
"ONE V, ONE…"
"Shom shut the hell up" Mike growled.
"Unable to shut required designation."
"Dharma, Dharma come here." Lukas beckoned to the one clinging to her brother "Come on, sit here." He got up ushering her to take his seat assisted with Arten's reassurance despite his mind being elsewhere. "Put your hand on this ball," Captain Griffin placed Dharma's right hand on a sphere partly embedded in the desk, "it's very sensitive, just move it around, get a feel for it."

Dharma's already large eyes widened further with nerves watching the image of a ship moving on the flight simulator responding to movements of the sphere at her highly sensitive fingertips. Although sheathed in gloves that could mimic a vice, micro sensors almost provided an extension of nerves from her own fingers. She turned to face Lukas at her side, shaking her head.

"You have to Dharma, we can't see where we are going, you can, follow the strongest current." Lukas put his arm around her shoulders.
"Him" She pointed at Jack who knelt on the floor next to Caron.
"We can't see like you Dharma." Jack's hand reached for the wall as things began to tilt again.

Dharma closed her eyes while Arten did his best to send calming thoughts to all of them. Her fingers gently moved the sphere. Lukas touched an indicator light overriding Shom's control of the ship before he was thrown backwards, the ship lurched and jumped as if being kicked underneath. Arten clung to the desk, now totally focused on keeping Dharma steady with telekinetic abilities; which would normally have people floating around. No this time like a rock he held her down while others endured the storm. Jack and Caron's limp body slid into a corner along with debris from Mike's over zealous fixing of things. Dharma saw the ship being tossed around, fighting to seek the right hand stream of light, away from the turbulent centre where the two streams fought for supremacy. A young inexperienced woman, like her brother; in many ways still a child, battled her own fears, she wanted to run, let someone else be responsible for the lives of everyone onboard, one slip of her fingers on the sphere would be catastrophic.

"Owww, no, hmmm, NO, owww"

Dharma tried and tried again, the ship so sluggish amidst rapidly changing currents. No sooner did she find a way than another surge of energy sent Argo rolling or off in another trajectory. She soon learnt that some colors were to be avoided; indicative of polarities that repelled or attracted the ship sending Argo off course again. Energy spikes licked the ship like a monster clawing at her hull. Brief, sudden moments of nothing, then slamming into waves of energy again. Engines screamed at her demanding commands draining power from already strained systems. Consoles flickered.

"Captain," Yoto's shaky voice called, "generator five reaching critical, six will blow with it and…" Lukas terminated the communication.

It really didn't matter, whether they lived or died was purely dependant on a pilot that had never flown so much as a kite before. Generators were surplus to requirements for a heap of space debris being fried by an electric and gravitational Hell as far as he was concerned. It was all or nothing. Dharma became part of what she could see, no longer a ship in a torrent, it was her gliding, seeking the right current, surfing waves instead of smashing against them, feeling the flow of power and polarity. Her terrified expression turned to glee, a child with a new toy.

"Dharma, Dharma, hello" Lukas waved a virtual hand in front of her shielded face.

"Hmmm" her eyes popped open, "I liked that, you try" she prodded Arten.

"Wow keep it steady!" Lukas felt rumblings as Argo slipped into turbulence again "I guess we're not out of the storm yet?"

"The streams part soon." Arten advised; his eyes closed to distractions.

"Shom calculate new ETA." Lukas looked around, still unnerved by creaking from the hull.

"Light speed approximately seventy two, course modification seven point eight, eight, five. New destination Sirius B. impact in thirty two hours fourteen minutes and seven seconds, WARN…"

"End report." Lukas swallowed hard and froze for a moment.

"I don't like the sound of that, I mean what happened to ARRIVAL, hope you had a pleasant flight an all!?" Jack looked from Mike to Lukas waiting for reassurance, Caron wasn't the only one who'd felt the cold touch of near death, in his case it had been the abyss of space that had nipped at his soul.

"Okay Special Ensign Dharma" Lukas spoke in the calmest voice he could muster.

"That doesn't give us time to slow down Captain we…" Mike had visions of Argo pate smeared lightly over Sirius B.

"Yes yes" Lukas waved at Mike to shut up. "Now Dharma… can you hear me" he looked up toward Arten.

"Yes Mr. Lukas" Dharma replied in a tone of being far away in a trance.

"I need you to look for a wave, or light that streams away from the main flow and kinda fades into space, can you do that?"

"Yes Mr. Lukas there is one ahead coming soon, I have to" the ship trembled for a few seconds "That's it I'm on a path to the wave now."

"Arten, see this blue indicator here" Lukas ushered him to the other working console.

"Yes Sir."

"As your Sister eases away from the main stream I want you to move your finger slowly down this blue line all the way to the bottom okay?"

"How slowly Sir?"

"Sync with your Sister, as the ship moves away and into the dark space, erm, well slide down the line as she slides along the wave."
"I see." Arten closed his eyes "Now?"
"Yes, erm." Lukas looked at Dharma wishing he could see what they could "Are you ready Dharma?"
"She says wait a moment Mr. Lukas" Arten replied.
"Well you two," Griffin swallowed hard again "sort it out."

Mike wondered if he should adopt a belief in God, he felt sure this was a damn good time to start praying as what the twins were attempting to do would normally involve the assistance of a very powerful computer making endless split second calculations. This was like sending a blind man through a field of banana skins, one slip and they were all space junk. Every moment that passed in a deathly silence seemed like an eternity.

"Mr. Lukas, there's a big rock, very big." Dharma knew there was no way she could steer around the thing and stay on the wave, her heart raced.
"Yoto, fire pulse cannons NOW!"
"At what? With what? I have no controls Captain!"
"Then kiss your ass goodbye" Lukas muttered to himself and closed eyes.

The mountain sized rogue asteroid slowly tumbled through space tens of thousands of miles away, minding it's own business. Argo a tiny dart seventy two times the speed of light closing that distance in seconds, riding an invisible wave, it's engine ports blazing a blue light arcing around Argo's semi circular stern, that gracefully flowed out into short wings furnishing massive port and starboard cannons. The Argo's figure curved back toward centre before straightening its lines; tapering to an arrow head shaped front. This class had been nicknamed the Axe head by engineers and artists alike. Light seemed to ripple over its surface as the Argo raced majestically toward its end, there was no cutting this rock with any axe. The silent crew held their breath as thunder filled their ears.

"EEEEWWWWWW" Dharma squealed as the asteroid loomed.

"Goodbye Captainnnnnn."

Shom's words faded. Just as humans use electrical impulses, like any biological organism she required power in order to function, power that Shom sacrificed. As if in slow motion bolts of light flashed from pulse cannons recoiling under the force. Rocks barely had a chance to smash against the ship's hull as Argo flew through the exploding asteroid. Suddenly Conference Room doors slid open a few inches. Lukas gently eased Arten's hand away from the gravity wave control that's blue line had vanished.

"We're OUT!?" Mike's face adopted a broad smile "We done it?"
"Well they did," Lukas gestured to the twins. "Shom half reverse thrusters."
"Shom, is, well dead Captain, systems will function under our control alone." Mike's smile seeped away.
"Right, of course." Lukas manipulated various readings, most of which displayed red "That should slow us without causing more damage. Dharma can you point us to the right of the diamond, about forty degrees?"
"Trying, its very…"
"Sluggish, I know. Just stick with it." Lukas patted her on the back, wanting to hug her but distracting the only pilot they had right now was not a good idea.
"I think that's about right," Dharma looked up and to her side at the Captain.
"Thank you Dharma, you deserve a medal, can you continue for a while, try to avoid any rocks out there?"
"Yes Sir."
"Okay guys we have a mess to clear up, I need to get down to the hanger deck."
"You should let the marines and engineers sort that out Sir." Mike suggested.
"No, I have friends down there… I hope."
"Droids might be better suited to the job Lukas." Mike felt uncomfortable about mentioning military secrets in present company.
"Okay, well let's assemble at the mess hall Mike you check deck three, gather anyone you find…"

"Captain," Jack interrupted.
"She's not here Mr. Lukas." Arten crouched over Caron.

Chapter Four: The Sirius Connection

"We have a few hours to get this ship operational again before entering the Sirius system." Lukas addressed assembled crew in a mess hall that presently lived up to its name. "Form teams, one engineer and two marines; Wayne, Tyler with Jasmine. Alan take Ursula and Rick. Ivan, Kerry…" He gestured to crew members, forming their teams. "Ivan I need you to track down and fix the sensor fault like yesterday. Jasmine, Tanya; take your teams to the Bridge. Alan, Kerry: assist Craig in engineering. Curtis, Mags, Brent, Mac, Sven, Anwar, Yun and Monique with me. The rest of you check every room, deck by deck, make reports on any structural or technical damage, clear up what you can. Okay people lets get to it."

"I hope your skills won't be needed Monique, but who knows what we'll find down there." Lukas led the group trotting along corridors of deck three.
"I haven't had a chance to check equipment in the medical centre Captain." Monique wondered if she'd make it down to the hanger at all, it had been many years since she'd trotted anywhere.
"You let technicians deal with that mess." Lukas gestured for her to enter a maintenance shaft others were drifting down into darkness of lower decks.
"I'm too old for these fun and games, oh, oh my." Monique stepped into the shaft, fell a few feet then shot upwards before managing to control her CAP unit.

Jack picked up a wooden chair, activating the console in Caron's quarters he sat down gingerly hoping he wouldn't break the old fashioned furnishing. It creaked slightly, as it was designed to do. He gazed over at the still figure laying beneath sheets drawn up to her neck. Caron's head rested deeply in soft pillows. Mike had speculated that she'd succumb to a self induced coma or trance, some form of reaction to trauma. Until the medical centre was up and running he couldn't investigate further. He'd set about that task while Jack watched over her, spending the last twenty minutes picking up books and numerous 'nick-knacks' that littered Caron's room. Arten had related what he'd perceived in her mind, darkness, the chill of death, water filling a small chamber. She'd let go, surrendered to her fate, more than that Arten could not see, there seemed to be nothing now, a void, within it somewhere Caron was lost.

Jack recalled his own living nightmare aboard the Logan Five space station that's main occupation was tracking terrorists and criminals. Their fate to languish in one of the moons mining facilities. However, Logan Five could only locate DNA of known terrorists, the one that managed to infiltrate the station only became known as he sabotaged Logan Five; killing himself and many of the crew. Jack remembered the explosion, why now, just as he was about to take six months leave. Five minutes and he'd have boarded a shuttle. Aware of cooling blood trickling down his face Jack sat up, but could move no further. Ringing in his ears muffled screams of others, though terror on their faces would be imprinted on his mind forever. The shuttle had ripped away from its docking, rupturing the port, sucking anyone, who couldn't hold on, out into space. Jack looked down, his mangled leg saved him from that fate, trapped as it was beneath a fallen maintenance module, it wouldn't be long though before air ran out. He watched helplessly as everything flew toward the ruptured airlock, at least some debris had built up, conspiring to block that gaping hole. He screamed in agony as the vacuum tried to claim him, tugging his body against the anchor of a broken, bleeding leg.

Vision started to blur, feeling cold replacing heat of searing pain. His eye caught sight of fiber optic cable and other object in the module. Grabbing cable he fought to tie it under arms and across his chest, unreeling a good twenty feet of cable Jack secured it to the module and searched its contents for something to use as a lever. He froze as lights flickered, if power went out then so would oxygen; already in short supply. Dammit, he couldn't find anything but gadgetry or things that just wouldn't come out of a gap he had access to. Finally Jack retrieved something; he stared at the laser cutter, then at the long rectangular module lying across his leg. Lights flickered again, leaving no choice, despite being wrenched by depressurization something had to be cut to get free. Jack pointed the device a foot to the right of his leg squeezing its trigger, hoping there was nothing explosive in the module. In moments the laser cut a jagged slice through the module, which fell in half. Jack hadn't enough feeling left to know if weight had eased off his leg, so cold he could barely move. Pushing backwards, kicking the module with his left leg, Jack broke free and grasped the seat he'd been thrown off. Hands turning blue pulled him along the row, grasping seat edges one by one. Reaching their end he was still nearly ten feet away from another airlock and fighting for breath. He eyed stanchions adjacent to the airlock, if he could just reach that, maybe nine feet.

Crawling off chairs, dragging a useless leg behind, Jack braced his good leg against the last seat pushing himself toward the stanchion, trying to remain steady, laying flat and stretching forward along the floor. The station listed, sections breaking off and rolling away from Logan Five's main hub. A loud creak followed by compartment doors bursting open released a hail of luggage flying toward the rupture, a container slammed into Jack's shoulder. He'd screamed, swore, cursed, thrown back catapulting into seats. A groan let out from the dieing station, another rupture vented air into space competing with the first. His grasp ripped from seats, Jack was thrown around in darkness, slamming into one thing or another, holding arms around his head, chest constricted by the cable he could do nothing. Time seemed to slow, his body swayed in a torrent of decompression though it all happened in slow motion. It was then he saw someone, something, blurred in the chaos. Jack called out for help to a misty light, whoever it was said something, he couldn't remember, something about 'other plans', it made no more sense than the feather gracefully drifting down before him. Delusional, his brain starved of oxygen, but he wasn't going to any damn light at the end of a tunnel just yet. Jack fought against Death, arm over arm pulling himself along the cable while ruptures competed for his corpse, sliding him from side to side over the deck. His hand made contact with the module, no, no it was a stanchion his arms now held. Dim lighting returned, localized emergency power, Jack looked up, the airlock, nearly there, can't quite reach control panel, he stretched, no, can't. Jack hoisted himself up the stanchion until he could kneel on one good knee with his back to it. He reached out to a blurred red light of the airlock control panel, nothing happened he tried, tried again, red, no green, green that was it, hit green.

"Help us, we, uhhh."
"Caron?" Jack wrenched from his memories by Caron's mumbling "Hey, girl, are you with us?" He stroked Caron's hair, sitting next to her on the bed.
"Must come, don't go, don't…" Her arms fought with the sheets, finally free a hand grasped Jack's arm, pulling him down before he had a chance to react. "Not again, don't leave me again…" Caron's voice expressed desperation, her arms thrown around Jack.
"I, err, I'm here" Jack could see Caron wasn't entirely, her eyes still closed and mind obviously elsewhere.
"Noo, I love…" Caron's grasp relaxed, eyes now open "Wha, where, where's he gone?" She sat up as did Jack.
"Erm, Spiderman?"
"What? Oh, fool." She slapped his leg.
"Who were you dreaming about, are you okay?"
"I," Caron looked away "yes I think so." Feeling her brow, Caron looked around wondering why she was in bed and more to the point why was Jack sitting on it, not that she would… well.
"I, we were worried about you there, you passed out, or something."
"Oh, oh garf yes, I never want that damn helmet on again, I can't, I just can't." Her knuckles turned white grasping sheets.
"I think you were okay until the visor turned opaque, you didn't know how to activate any of the visual modes and…"
"The darkness, I can't… take that." Caron shivered. "I was trapped once, nearly died, in fact I still don't know how the sub…"

--*--

Helmet lights darted about as engineers and marines cautiously opened hatches sealing most of deck one off from the rest of Argo. For all the different modes of seeing technology could provide, in circumstances like these they preferred what eyes could naturally perceive. Fortunately it was not an area usually frequented by crew, most of it containing Raven class interceptors and other craft stored out of sight. Interceptors were launched from tubes adjacent to the main bay, only shuttles and craft returning occupied space on the hanger deck. To what extent outer bay doors had buckled they had no idea yet, but without an operational launch/landing bay there would be no exploring. Argo itself could not attempt a landing with a breach in her hull. Helmet lights now streamed into a corridor as hatch doors were manually rolled back.

"Sven, go back and check rooms, storage, anywhere someone may be trapped." Lukas ordered.
"We can activate droids from here Captain." Curtis reminded, preferring to send a machine into the bay rather than risk themselves.
"Zack, anyone?" The Captain tried calling in vain.

Alien alloy that Argo had been constructed with blocked com signals, it was thought to be part of a stealth system, though scientists could never work out how to make that system fully functional. Instead it left ship designers and engineers with a problem in that the only way to communicate with other areas of these ships was through hardwired systems, virtually taking technology back to the twenty first century. Without power the team had left a trail of relay transmitters to keep in touch with deck three.

"Hello?" Helmet lights all focused on one spot as another beam of light entered the corridor.
"Hey! What kept you?" Grant walked toward them.
"Just the usual ship destroying catastrophes that happen when McThug doesn't get his oats in the morning!" Maggie taunted a large muscular marine standing next to her.
"Och its justa pilot, throw him back." McThug, as he was known, slapped Grant on the back. "And as fer yew, wee haggis, there's neh enough meat on yer bones fer a snack." his giant stature towered over 'the wee haggis', aka Maggie.
"Ooh I thought you were fond of my dumplings!" She wiggled.
"Alright enough! Damn marines can't take you anywhere… Twice."

"I… err thought you were a marine… Captain?" Curtis dared to venture, his comment replied to with a very marinish filthy look.
"What's the situation on the deck Pilot?" Lukas was in no mood for marine banter.
"Maintenance crew were trying to fix an intermittent fault between inner and outer launch bay doors; outer not acknowledging that inner were closed, presumed to be a fault on inner door sensors."
"You were screwing around with that three days ago!"
"Ya it's been an endless session of launch sequences, shuttle inner bay, outer bay, inner bay, outer bay, it was Zack's turn to play yoyo… He was in there when the shit hit the fan."
"So there's a shuttle in the outer bay?"
"Yes Sir, we were thrown around, then a deafening boom, power went out, Yakov and I came here and activated Beta droids to go check things out."
"The hatches were working?"
"No, some we yanked open with no problem, others like this one seemed welded shut, couldn't budge them." Grant gestured to the hatch. "Power returned briefly, inner bay doors screeched closed behind the shuttle. Yakov, Mo, the droids and someone else made it through before they closed though. Power went out again so I started back to grab Delta droids, power came back on, I turned back. Power went off and on again, so I though to hell with it get the Delta's, then all hell broke loose, I heard another boom, yelling, the hatches closed. Tried to restore power, but the whole zone is dead Captain, sorry I don't know much more than that."
"So we have a bunch of people and a shuttle trapped in the outer bay?"
"Yes Sir as far as I know."
"The inner bay is pressurized then?"
"Yes just need to get that hatch open, if power returns though there's no guarantee that the inner bay doors won't open."

Lukas's group made preparations while waiting for a status report from other areas of the ship, conscious that time was running short. Dharma still piloted Argo, complaining of being tired and not able to focus for much longer. Certain that power would not be returned to lower decks until orders were given, the team rigged up a portable power unit to the interlocking double reinforced bay hatch.

"Give it a jolt," Lukas steadied himself, if the bay had depressurized there would be one hell of a vacuum trying to attract their attention.
"We're good," Curtis peered through a small gap between the now unsealed doors.
"Okay open them up, let's get in there." Brent gestured at Yun to power the doors again.

--*--

"Ahh your back in the land of the living I see." Mike dropped by to check on Caron, who had a mug of tea in one and a Jack hand in the other.
"If you can call this living, I guess." Caron wore a solemn expression after the pair had shared their near death stories.
"Well things are fitting back together, and we'll be orbiting some kinda rock soon." he tried a smile "You might even be able to get your hands dirty!"
"Oh, is that legal these days?" Caron glared.
"How are you feeling?"
"Okay, I'll be fine."
"Right, well I'll be getting back to my super glue and sticky tape then." Mike, feeling somewhat unwelcome, left Caron in Jack's capable hands.
"So you were saying about the light, or whatever, spoke to you." Caron steered the conversation with Jack back on course.
"Yeah, probably just delusional, head injury, leg was bleeding pretty bad too, can't have been much oxygen in there, lucky I got out at all."
"I know the feeling" Caron sipped her tea as a distraction from pain of her memories "no shape to the light then?"
"No, vaguely human, but time can alter memories." He smiled and laughed "Could have sworn I saw a feather, like I say, the ol brain was loosing it."
"A feather?" Caron sat up from her slouch.
"Yeah, a large luminescent white feather, like anything would be floating around!"

"That's… odd" Caron's free hand seemed to place itself over her heart without conscious direction. "it, was it like an ostrich feather?"

"No idea, guess it was a bit fancy, I only saw it for a second, it blurred and vanished with the light, but hey could have been a purple penguin for all the sense anything made at the time, ya know." Jack finished his coffee.

"Pass me that book." Caron pointed at a shelf Jack had stacked various items on.

"This one?"

"No the green one… there that's it."

"The Legacy of Gods." He read aloud before handing it to her "Interesting read?"

"Yes you could say that." she fanned through pages, turning a few more; finding an illustration. "Did it look like that?"

"Err," Jack squinted "yeah… actually and that's…"

"Thoth, you were being weighed my dear fellow." Caron stared at the image of Thoth holding scales, on one side a feather on the other a heart. "Judged, 'other plans' you said… right?"

"I think so yes, but…" Jack looked disturbed, uneasy as if someone had walked over his grave.

"I was shown a heart" Caron thought aloud.

"You didn't mention that."

"It never seemed relevant before." Her voice softened by far away thoughts.

"So what does that all mean?"

"I'm not sure." Caron pulled back sheets and stood up, there was far more she hadn't revealed and wasn't about to "Well lets get something done, can't sit around all day or night, or whatever it is."

--*--

Lukas eyed a row of metallic eggs ranging in size from Delta tennis balls up to Alpha's about four feet high in their present inactive state. He reached forward touching a green light on one three foot high egg nestled into a wall cavity. Pressure locks released the morphing droid which unfolded arms, legs and a head adopting a classic robotic appearance.

"What's your name droid?"
"Beta zero four seven, Spanner Sir."
"That's all we need, a spanner in tha works!" McThug laughed at yet another of his not so funny jokes.
"You so funnie, you making my head huwt" Yun pointed to the side of her helmet.
"Aye, maybe if I squish yew an wee haggis here together, we can make one proper big person, short stuff. I thought three feet was tha minimum height fer marines?"
"Maybe we take you head off we find some wee noodles!" Yun stuck her tongue out, not that anyone could see it with her helmet activated.
"Oh for heaven's sake, why do we need more kids in the world when we've got marines!" Lukas rolled his eyes.
"He st…." Yun pointed at McThug.
"DON'T you even THINK about saying he started it, or I'll put you over my knee and spank your butt!"
"Ohhh but he…" Maggie stood with a hand on her hip batting her eyelashes at the Captain.
"Shut it." Anwar commanded.
"Thank you Lieutenant, now can we get in there children?" Lukas gestured to the hatch. "Okay Spanner, with me."
"With you sir?" Spanner stood motionless.
"Follow me." Lukas sighed.

Night vision revealed a bay in good shape. Reverting to torchlight again they moved quickly to a shuttle that's cockpit lights illuminated part of the bay. A relieved Rhianna was found at the helm, though could add little to what Grant had told them while Monique checked her over.

"Okay Spanner search for any loose objects in the hanger, stow them away and report to me when done."
"Yes Sir" Spanner hovered away.
"Yun seal the bay hatch, Rhianna see if you can get power down here, we'll use the airlock to enter the bay once those doors are open, give us at least ten minutes from now. Yun go with her, seal the hatch behind you and wait there."

The bright Sirius A star became a ball rather than a distant bright point of light to the naked eyes that were momentarily distracted on Argo's Bridge. The image brought relief as sensors were back online and officers could resume control. With a few false starts and further repairs power returned to Argo's hanger deck and with it an ability to see the outer launch bay. Crew waited with heavy hearts in a shuttle while the main hanger depressurized. No one really expected to find any survivors amidst the frozen carnage that greeted their eyes. Magnetic forces of launch and landing bays provided an invisible buffer in what was essentially a large rectangular airlock. With the power cut and Argo out of control shuttle three had crashed down impacting the deck, then it and any crew, were thrown around inside the launch area. While suits provided a lot of protection, there was little that could prevent being crushed by a shuttle smashing against walls.

"I'd say the doors started to open, power went out, when it came back on they attempted to close, in the meantime shuttle three's helm wedged in the gap." Brent speculated.
"Are the outer doors operational now? Lukas queried.
"No, analysis shows some major mechanical damage, easy enough to replace those parts when we can get at them, but..." Curtis gleaned from another console.
"Any reading on life signs yet?"
"No but with that thing smashing around in there it could have damaged sensors." Brent clung to fading hope.
"Probably better to wait until the ship is stationary before we attempt anything Captain, there's no..." Anwar tried to suggest.
"WAIT..." Brent signaled for everyone to shut up, adjusting settings on a console. "Come in... can you read me?" he listened intently but shook his head. "Sorry thought for a minute I...."
"Cauccchhh i..."
"Curtis, Thug and Anwar with me, Monique do you have any experience with this kinda situation?"
"Not really Luke, and I'm a bit old for flying around in there!"
"Okay." Although Lukas would prefer to have medical assistance on hand, he knew it was a bit much to ask of Monique in the circumstances. "Lets get in there, whoever it is they must be in that

shuttle."

Spanner joined them gliding along the launch channel toward a badly damaged Hawk class shuttle, 'shuttle' being a diplomatic term for a troop transporter and very much a heavily armed predator. Its flight appearance being similar to the Argo with more distinct crescent shaped wings, splaying out from a Hawk's main body when entering planetary atmospheres or combat. This left the main transport 'body' tapering a more slender 'neck' to the bow or 'head' of the craft. In its present state the shuttle had an oval appearance if viewed from above. Approaching, as they were from behind it might be best described as white lips pouting engine ports. The helm locked in icy jaws of the outer bays doors, leaving a wide slit of space visible, which had claimed anything loose in the launch bay.

"Spanner, remove obstruction and activate airlock door" Curtis hovered over the upper docking port gazing down at a trail of frozen blood blurring control panel light beneath.
"Clearing" Spanner scanned and then melted blood, which floated up in bubbles rapidly freezing again, "Port activated, warning airlock occupied."
"Someone's in there?" Lukas drifted to Spanners side.
"Unknown Sir."
"Well access port control and analyze stupid!" Curtis rebuked.
"No life signs present, visual." Spanner projected an image of the airlocks contents.
"Oh frag that's Vern." Curtis looked away from an image of Vern crumpled at the airlock's inner hatch, arm severed at his shoulder.
"Can't imagine how he made it in there, but he didn't last much longer." Thug commented.
"Remove image, decompress and open airlock Spanner. Thug take Vern back to the main hanger will you." Lukas watched as the former technician froze and started to float. "Err, bring Brent and Maggie back with you."
"Yes Sir" McThug grasped Vern with one hand, manipulating CAP controls with another he jetted away.
"Let's get in there, Spanner you wait here and control the airlock." Lukas descended into the blood stained airlock followed by Curtis

and Anwar.

"Either the fuselage is buckled or something's jamming it in there," Curtis stamped his foot down on the inner airlock hatch, which gradually relented under a creaking protest to reveal a devastated transport area; floor and walls buckled.

"Anyone here?" Anwar's helmet lights highlighted cables hanging from the ceiling, panels and other debris lying over and amidst seating rows, internal compartments crumpled, stanchions bent or fallen.

"We still have air pressure Sir," Curtis checked readings on his forearm.

"This bird will never fly again," Lukas's helmet lights peered into dimly lit areas "Can't see any…" his words stopped by the sound of metal hitting metal to the stern.

"Over there, generator access hatch." Curtis scrambled over seats, throwing debris to the side, eventually reaching a hatch which had no power. "Definitely someone in there." Again something impacted the hatch's other side. "Room service." He grabbed a piece of twisted metal hitting the hatch three times. "Guess I didn't see the 'do not disturb' sign!" Curtis froze as electricity crackled all over his suit.

"You're standing on a power coupling" Lukas pointed to the floor.

"Oh shit," Curtis stepped back "Must be something live in this wall as well." He watched electricity dance over its surface before dissipating. "Can't harm us, but it may have fused this hatch, virtually welded the damn thing!"

"I thought this alloy was tough?" Lukas gazed around at carnage.

"It has odd properties Captain, extremely high melting point, but becomes more like steel at room temperature, so unless its part of the outer hull it can buckle under extreme forces." Curtis gestured to walls behind them. "Actually it's the seals that would have fried rather than the door itself, so all…."

"…ator dischhhhhhhh…"

"Repeat." Lukas concentrated.

"….cchhhharge."

"Static, caused by static?" Curtis suggested.

"Ator, dis, discharge, generator discharge!" Lukas concluded "crap that's not good, we gotta shut it down."

"Yeah right, give me a week!" Curtis looked around at cables

hanging from ceiling and walls, burnt out consoles "not even sure if… yeah I guess there must be some connection as lights over there are still working, maybe… no" he thought aloud trying to fathom some way to shut generators down from this part of the ship.
"Helm controls might still work." Lukas suggested.
"No way of getting to that, this end of the bird is bad enough the helm must be fit for the junkyard reaper!"
"Won't know until we look."
"Look! Captain the helm's been smashed by bay doors, half of its hanging outside, get sucked out there and its goodbye Kansas." Curtis spoke as if the Captain had lost his mind.
"Age before beauty" Maggie commented with her foot on McThug's helmet, assisting his decent into hell.
"Wow, why waz I neh invited ta this parteh!?" McThug gazed around until he felt Maggie's boot in his rear; her gentle way of saying 'get the heck outta my way'.
"Oh great here comes the circus!" Curtis muttered.
"Yeah, clowns assist Curtis. Brent check the forward hatch." Lukas pointed to the oval door.
"Och I'll neh get Castle Age weh this." McThug threw a broken virtual entertainment visor over his shoulder.
"Seems fine Captain." Brent examined hatch controls.
"Compression in the corridor?"
"Err, yep."
"Okay you guys hold the fort, I'll check it out."

Lukas, ignoring protests about safety and duty of his rank, entered a passage leading to the helm, sealing the hatch behind him. Other than familiar damage the passage seemed to be structurally fine at one end, the far end told another story. An upper girder, running the passage length like a spine, had succumb to massive pressure from launch bay doors; bending circular ribs inward with it and narrowing the passage considerably in front of the cockpit's hatch. Lukas crouched, taking a moment to assess the situation. He faced two dilemmas; firstly if he got to the hatch would it open, and secondly; given the damage here what state would the cockpit be in. He could have sent Spanner up here, but more than anything Lukas wanted to find Zack still alive. Zack's Father; Josh, had saved his life on more than one occasion, Lukas promised to watch over Josh's Son, now Zack, a mere nineteen year old, was almost certainly dead. Lukas's gut turned at the thought of bringing that news to the boy's father.

Cautiously navigating through the birds snapped neck hearing air hissing out from a fracture, he reached the hatch. Moving debris obstructing its control panel, Lukas tried to make sense of pressure levels and various other data the panel provided. It all made perfect sense to an engineer, that was not his strong point. Making a promise to himself to spend more time with technicians if he survived this, Lukas touched the open icon, but hatch doors simply clunked each time he tried. With a pounding heart he synchronized kicking doors while pressing the icon. He wanted a sure grasp on something rather than throwing himself at them, as the cockpit was almost certainly claimed by the vacuum of space. One slip and he'd be gone. The thought that perhaps they could slow Argo down, come back and find him before he starved to death crossed Lukas's mind as the hatch suddenly gave. He fell backward grasping at anything, but no vacuum attempted to rip him out into the void.

"Still have pressure up here, just about." Releasing his grip Lukas stood up, cautiously entering a partly crushed cockpit, surprised to see warning indicators blinking in its darkness.
"Power?" Curtis hoped.
"Yeah," Lukas moved carefully toward instrument panels, air escaped through another rupture, and a creak did nothing to improve his confidence. "Shit!" He grasped at the copilots seat as the helm shuddered.
"Captain?" Anwar called.
"Yeah yeah I'm okay, controls at least partially operational, trying to get at them, bit tight in here… shit, Zack, Zack, hey buddy." Lukas grasped an arm he'd almost stepped on, jutting out from beneath helm controls.
"You found him boss?" Maggie wanted to know good or bad news, waiting being the worst part of life or death situations.
"Think so, yeah it's Zack, he's still alive, barely." Lukas checked readings on Zack's wrist. "He's trapped under a ton of crap, looks

like the cockpit caved in on the pilots side. Air is leaking. Get that droid up here now before this mess disintegrates.

"Can you find generator readings Captain?" Brent signaled for Maggie to get the droid.

"Looking" his eyes darted around, while aware of a hiss that's tone seemed to have a hollow pitch now, "Hang in there kid." He knelt up surveying controls on the navigator's side, fingers tapping a small display. "Where's that frackin droid?"

"Coming through the airlock Sir," Maggie replied.

"There are two active generators, let me know if the lights go out in there, is that droid in yet?" Lukas became more agitated by rattling and creaking around him.

"Yes Sir." Brent's hand reached for hatch controls.

"Send him in here." Lukas heard the hatch open and close again

"Okay here goes." He tapped a red icon beneath one of two glowing sphere icons.

"We still have power Sir." Curtis responded.

"Hmm, okay I'll…."

"Guys my leg is trapped, the generators down, but I'm kinda stuck…. Can you hear me?"

"Yeah coming through Sonya, are you anywhere near the hatch?" Curtis felt a sense of relief.

"No, blow the damn thing open if you have to!"

"You getting this Captain?" Anwar checked.

"Yes great, get her out of there ASAP." Lukas turned his attention to the droid. "What are you doing?"

"Repairing hatch Sir" Spanner replied to the dismayed Captain "Error correction, repair complete."

"Well that's just dandy are we ready for take off now!? Get your metal ass in here, analyze damage here and formulate the safest way to remove personnel from this position." Lukas changed com frequencies to remove marine chatter about blowing up hatches and not being so stupid 'you great turnip'.

"Analyzing status Sir," Spanner scanned wreckage, visibly apparent by a yellow beam flowing over the twisted technological carcass above Zack. "Will require cutting section seven and eight and removal of damaged apparatus Sir."

"Right get to it then." Lukas gestured, wishing he could just get on with it himself.

"Unable to comply, operation would endanger personnel."
"I'll endanger your… What's the problem, why isn't it safe?"
"Removal of damaged apparatus may alter structural integrity of cockpit. Live cables still present. Recommend depressurization and termination of power supply Sir."
"Look can you move some of this crap, we can't cut the power just yet."
"Removing auxiliary components." Several of Spanner's lasers began slicing and dicing anything that wasn't structural or live, ripping loose objects away, throwing them to the side using a telescopic tentacle that's tip extended into three claws.
"Easy there clankboy!" Lukas wondered what he'd unleashed and this wasn't even an Alpha droid. "Curtis have you got Sonya out of there yet?"
"No sir." Curtis wanted to make some comment about not being God an all, but thought better of it "Cutting hatch seals… no we're through."
"This yer idea o decorating lass!" McThug crouched next to Sonya, hanging out of a wall, her lower half caught in a narrow access shaft, crushed before she could get out of it.
"Can I have an intelligent life form in here please!" Sonya was in no mood for joking, even though she presently felt like one.
"Grief whatcha doing in there girl!?" Curtis couldn't help but laugh at the sight, Sonya was never going to live this one down.
"Okay let's just cut through here and Thug support her weight would you." He began the arduous task of cutting a girder with lasers.
"Get your hand off my butt you deranged creep." Sonya complained.
"Jus supporting tha vast majority of yer weight missy!" McThug grinned.
"Can't you," Maggie tilted her head "kinda twist her out of there?" she gestured a rolling motion.
"Hmm," Curtis stood back and examined the situation again. "Give it a try I guess."
"What's going on Brent?" Lukas's patience was running out after listening to Sonya screaming and then cursing everyone.
"Legs busted up Sir, but we're moving her into the airlock now."
"Find anyone else in there?"

"No sir."

"Okay, get everyone out I want to decompress the shuttle before I get blown out of here by some almighty fart."

"Yes Sir." Brent wondered what suicidal plan the Captain was attempting this time.

"Wrong end o tha ship Cap'n." McThug advised.

"An almighty belch then, I didn't know you were so technically minded Thug."

"Och only when it counts Sir, good luck." McThug stepped into a gravity well and looked up at Maggie waiting in the airlock. "Och tis a fine eve fer butt gazing."

"Finally the circus left town." Lukas muttered, setting controls to reduced pressure. "Just hold it together." He gazed around, nerves frayed by movement from the cockpit floor. "C'mon, gonna die of old age in here for craps sake." Pressure readings slowly fell, like a water tank emptying the bright blue indicator fell to seventy percent, sixty nine percent.

As if the mighty god of impatience had answered his call, serving espresso death, a chunk of fuselage tumbled into space. Lukas grasped what he could, his body flaying around. Activating Titan mode he began pulling himself toward the hatch with the cockpit disintegrating around him. The rush of air dissipated as he made it back into the passage, he turned, but there was no Spanner and no Zach, just skeletal remains of a cockpit.

"I tried Zack, I tried." Lukas slammed his fist into the closing hatch.

Chapter Five: Mysteries and monsters

"Who designed this bucket of shit Mike?" Mike experienced the lash of Lukas's tongue as the Captain stormed along corridors of deck four toward the Bridge.
"She was built over two hundred years ago Sir. Recent refits haven't exactly had much of a trial and the skill pool of those working on her wasn't exactly extensive."
"Remind me to shoot them if we ever get back."
"Sorry to hear about Zack." Mike, aware of Lukas's military connection to Zack's father, felt like he was walking on eggshells.
"Yeah, Yakov, Mohamed, Vern and Larann too, we rely too much on technology, even the ships brain is dead."
"I think we're all lucky to be alive Sir."
"That's… true Mike, I guess you're right." Lukas entered the Bridge "How's Caron?"
"Doing fine, she's up and about." Mike was glad of the focus on good news.
"She and Jack need some basic training, arrange that when things settle down. Okay Yoto how are things shaping up?" Lukas noted wires still hanging from terminals.
"Your command station will be operational soon Captain, we have restored navigation, weapons, tactical, one generator is causing a few hold ups, com channels are still out in a few areas but that's being attended to."
"Struc…" Lukas suddenly felt strange, as if his body had immersed in the relaxing heat of a hot tub, yet he felt as light as air, the knot in his stomach untwisted.
"Sir?" Yoto stared at him, the Captain appeared to have slipped into a trance, gazing across the Bridge at nothing.
"No." An image of Arten appeared and faded, morphing into Zack within Lukas's mind.
"Are you okay Sir?" Mike hovered awkwardly, removing a medical scanner from his belt.
"Yeah, I, have Zack… Arten report to the Bridge will you." Lukas rubbed his temple.
"I'd like you to get checked out Captain." Mike couldn't find

anything to worry about on his scanner, but the Captain's vagueness wasn't a good sign.

Monique monitored surgical progress as Sonya lay unconscious in a cylinder with her leg opened up by little robotic tools, working faster than a human eye could follow. Other weird looking mechanisms that would frighten the pants off anyone if viewed under a microscope, reconstructed Sonya's shattered knee cap. This was only Monique's third space flight, others being no more than short trips to the Mars station, so although she was getting on for two hundred and fifty years old, there was a great deal to get used to, such as the suits and CAP units. Even having so many young people running around was a novelty, though such reminded Monique of her own age. She made a mental note to check whether all crew members had been offered longevity. The process was far from perfect, at her age fatigue was a constant burden, her research into that continued whenever she'd time to spare. Gazing up at the sound of medical centre doors opening Monique screamed as only someone could in utter terror. Oh she'd seen some gruesome sights in her career but this thing looked like one of the little monsters fixing Sonya's knee right now, only worse.

"HEEEEELLLP MEEEEEE, NAAAOOO, NO GET BACK, PLEE…." Monique screamed over the com, stumbling backwards she scrambled to find a safe place.
"Monique what the hells wrong?" Lukas snapped out of his daze.
"It's eating someone, it's in there." She sobbed. "It's in the lab, Sonya's in there, oh frag."
"Marines will be there any second, what is it, what's in there?" Lukas stood up, surrounded by crew on the Bridge equally confused and shocked.
"It's a huge spider like thing, please hurry I can hear it moving around in there, this door wont stop it." Monique hid in the changing cubical "AAAAAAAHHHHHHH, AAAHHHH." She heard a body being dragged, metallic scratching sounds against floor and equipment.
"What the hell, Anwar, are you there yet?" Lukas didn't know whether to run or wait for marines to do their job; staying put in an emergency was not an instinctive reaction for him.

"Armed and… what!" Anwar started laughing.
"Oh God it's got meh Sir arggg neh, neh mercy!" McThug coughed and choked.
"Oh you woss, ill handle the monster, you go run to Mummy." Maggie stepped forward.
"STOP screwing around WHAT is going on?" Lukas growled.
"It's a droid Sir, looks damaged, oh crap Zack's on the slab." Anwar revealed.
"Wha… Monique, that's a Beta droid, not some alien in your lab, get back in there." Lukas ran out of the Bridge.
"I'm in Captain sorry, I've never seen one of those… things." She emerged from her hiding place, eyeing the droid that had morphed into a crab like appearance in order to grasp what it could and carry the injured pilot as Spanner fought to re-enter the ship.
"Is he alive?" McThug grimaced at the twisted figure Monique scanned.
"Barely, spine broken, multiple breaks and fractures, internal bleeding, can, can someone remove that thing." Monique gazed over at the broken Spanner sprawled on her floor.
"Insofi… pooowwwwer lev…" Spanners lights dimmed.
"Och c'mear yer botty hero, I'll take yeh to tha Botty Doctor." McThug gathered up the mass of Spanner's gangly body, almost impacting the high velocity Captain while carrying Spanner out.
"What's..?"
"Spanner Cap'n." McThug strided off toward engineering.
"Can you…"
"Yes Luke I'll do my best." Monique retracted Zack's helmet before lowering the surgical shell. "Scare me like that again and I'll be conducting some genetically modified Captain experiment, took fifty years off my life that did, my heart still…."
"I'll just…" Lukas began backing away toward the medical centre's hatch.
"Can't take things like that at my age you know. I shall be lodging an official…" Monique's own version of metal and claws began to unveil.

--*--

Caron sat in a corner of the science lab reading simulated books, refreshing her extensive knowledge of a complex ancient world. An immense jigsaw puzzle of beliefs, art, mythology, sciences and languages. So many parts of that puzzle were missing, others often fitted together, yet like any jigsaw; pieces may fit but the picture doesn't. Academics had proposed various theories as being fact while conveniently missing out certain details that might contradict their so called facts. Caron attempted to play detective with evidence, facts not opinions, though matters were always open to interpretation. She admired the same qualities in Jack and what's more he was quite attractive really, lean, broad shoulders and obviously intelligent. Her gaze returned to pages, her mind grudgingly followed. Her heart, well that was more complex.

"Do we have any DNA samples from the Sumerian civilization?" Caron's revision had confirmed more than she suspected.
"We do," Jack, sitting at a central console, accessed files relating to her question "and… it looks like our prime suspect has gone out of his way to preserve the evidence."
"How so?" Caron looked up from her book, confirming that his face was strong too, intense in some respects. "Hmm…" Her mind wandered.
"They were obtained from the inside of sealed jars and… whatever they called jars back then. Why?"
"Sumerian civilization is older than Egyptian and from them we have this." Caron held up the book "The oldest story ever told. It's a mythical tale of King Gilgamesh."
"Yeah, rings a bell, big guy with an axe?" Jack attempted to demonstrate he wasn't completely ignorant in the myth department.
"That's the one, he was said to be two parts god and one part human, endowed with beauty by Shamash a SUN god, while his strength and courage endowed by Adad a STORM god. Sound familiar?"
"Sirius A and B?"
"Exactly, but the gods grew tired of Gilgamesh's arrogant and promiscuous ways. They sent a being to put him in his place." Caron smiled "This being had an ape like appearance."
"Like some depictions of Thoth?"
"Yep, but that's just the beginning. Enkidu, Thoth as we know

him, was educated by a priestess about the ways of man, and….
Sex," she shifted uncomfortably "perhaps this has more to do with human behavior, relationships, reproduction, even genetics." Caron steered away from lust to logic. "The priestess may have represented mother nature and Enkidu learning about Earth."
"So he's an alien from Sirius?"
"Well it seems he's sent to Earth from there."
"Hmm, why not just say that instead of all the poetry?"
"Oh well, gotta make a story entertaining, you know; scandal, heroes…"
"Sex."
"Yes, they were fond of that to… so I'm told." Caron grinned, hiding a flutter. "However, in my opinion it's the poetry that led to polytheist belief systems and… Anyway at this time Gilgamesh had a vision in which he's captivated, drawn to a heavy star that cannot be lifted despite his divine strength and that the star has a potent essence. Now the story related that this star descends from heaven to him and is the God of heaven. Obviously if a star hit the Earth there wouldn't be anything left of the planet to worry about, some interpretations speak of a meteor, but also that this IS Enkidu! So I think its reasonable to assume that this is Enkidu, god or perhaps Master of the heavens, in terms of knowledge, arriving on a space ship from a star that's almost certainly Sirius B."
"So we have an arrival date for Mr Thoth then?"
"Difficult to say, these stories are handed down from one culture to another, the story of Noah and the Ark came from the Sumerians for example, so this could all be from even older civilizations that have left little for us to investigate. Trying to do that nearly cost me my life as you know."
"Yes, Atlantis can stay where it is or maybe. "Jack raised an eyebrow at lives being lost on a big maybe. "Sirius seems ever more a certainty, but Mike feels that this system is far too young for life to have evolved here."
"We are constantly proven wrong by the stars from what I gather," Caron frowned at science's ego.
"True, very true."
"Anyway there is conflict between Gilgamesh and Enkidu, they sort things out though and become friends. Later in the story Enkidu dies which doesn't fit in with the ol immortal bit. It does

say that Gilgamesh also finds this difficult to believe and watches over the body for seven days after which a worm crawls from Enkidu's nose confirming…"

"A worm?" Jack sat straight, as if offended by something.

"Yes, although this might be open to interpretation somewhat," Caron noted Jack's stance.

"I would say so. Various species of insect take care of corpses, but worms are not one of them, not at that stage and not until the body is buried."

"Well it's said that a worm emerged from the egg and became a new Phoenix in another legend. However, that worm was actually a serpent symbolizing… other stuff, cutting a long story short snakes represented Earthly wisdom in ancient times" Caron didn't want to get into a long distracting conversation. "On that note though; later in the story, when Gilgamesh is searching for immortality, a snake steals a sacred herb from him, which rejuvenates, the snake sheds its skin blah, blah."

"The DNA retrieval, reforming… perhaps the dispute between Gilgamesh and Enkidu was more about keeping secrets of the gods or whatever these beings are." Jack proposed.

"Yes the gods were displeased that Gilgamesh was sowing his seed amongst humans, although it sounds like he's a hybrid."

"Perhaps Enkidu was going through a transformation rather than Death?"

"Yes, in fact death is only one of many transformations in mystical terminology, our entire bodies are replaced every two years if I remember correctly, so how many times have we died in this life, physically speaking." Caron parked herself on the desk next to Jack.

"We are infants really aren't we, I mean these guys were traveling between stars thousands, millions of years ago and we are knocking around in this old bucket." Jack reflected.

"Do you know what Gilgamesh named his old bucket?" Caron grinned.

"Not The Argo!?"

"Ohhh yes, a celestial ship that appears later in Greek legends too."

"Jason and the argonaughts!" Jack laughed.

"Crewed by fifty men who were all said to be related to Gilgamesh and in Greek legends were imbued with divine powers, some say

the Argo had propulsion systems, artificial intelligence, or Hera's divine guidance, it didn't even need a crew to fly."
"Well fifty oarsmen related to the number of years it takes Sirius B to orbit Sirius A I would imagine, as for our crew having divine powers though!" Jack laughed.
"Oh rain on my parade why don't you! Actually we have two angels, a hero or two and perhaps those who carry the favor of the gods." Caron gazed at Jack who felt awkward in the silence.
"Ha, well don't look at me!"
"The feather you saw represents truth, if it balances the scales a soul passes into the heavens as it were."
"But I didn't die."
"No, 'other plans', Enkidu didn't die either. Your feather fell, and you are in the heavens, so to speak."
"Okay then what does the heart mean?"
"It, it is devoured by some hellish monster… from the depths if the feather rises, meaning the heart is laden with guilt."
"The depths, you… And if the feather falls?"
"Then perhaps the heart is empty barren... Thoth was the Master of balance, balance is the key to life, unbalanced as humanity is, there's no spark of life, we are unable to bare children, until the truth is found."
"That's what the image was all about in your book? This is starting to creep me out."
"Well kinda, it's more a case of relating principles, concepts, and ethics." Caron deployed vagueness to avoid discussing other insights on the matter.
"Perhaps the heart rising represents innocence, no guilt, virginal, like a child…" Jack suggested, thwarting Caron's attempts at avoidance.
"Yes maybe going that way, sort of thing." Caron gestured as if pushing something to one side, while unconsciously crossing her legs. "Anyway the Argo in Greek mythology was a gift from Hermes."
"The Greek Thoth!"
"Who named this ship?"
"The Argo was named…" Jack accessed history of their ship, trying not to be overly distracted by Caron's thigh resting close to the display; casting a sheen of light over the deep blue uniform,

emphasizing her shapely hip. "The eagle class vessel SD 003 was named Argo in 2121 by HA! Your not gonna believe this; Jason Gilga, Chief biocom technician." Jack accessed software very familiar to him.
"He could be our man, he could still be on Earth, in Stasis." Caron leant around peering at the screen, steadying herself with a hand on Jack's shoulder.
"NO trace, there's no trace of his DNA, that's impossible." Jack expressed annoyance.
"Secret records?"
"Captain…"
"Jack." Lukas replied on his way back to the Bridge.
"I need security clearance to personnel that worked on these ships, I…."
"There is no security clearance Jack, you have full access."
"Shit, err, okay." Jack returned to tracing anything he could on Jason Gilga. "Well he left Research and Development a few years later, after then there's no trace of him."
"He wasn't put into Stasis?" Caron questioned.
"No record of it, not under that name anyway."
"If he worked on these ships then maybe there's some trace of him here?"
"Yes!.. Although he wiped out any records concerning his DNA or more likely the government did, maybe those who knew too much about these bio computers and military whatever were excluded from any records." Jack huffed.
"What's the problem?" Lukas stepped into the science lab, noting Jack and Caron's close proximity to each other.
"Can't find any trace of the guy I mentioned, think he may have been Thoth, but without DNA it's very likely he knew about mythology and given his name, he named this ship Argo." Jack explained.
"No trace?" Lukas felt frustrated that his experts had been hampered by a lack of information that should be there.
"Nothing, no DNA info from Earth, Mars… Hmm, where were these ships built? Actually I need a mobile tracker, is that…"
"Won't work on this ship, well it would take a week. Bring up the software." Lukas gestured to Jack's console, while walking past to the equipment storage: removing a Delta droid nestled in the wall.

"This little guy should do the trick." he placed the bronze sphere into a glowing bowl shaped receptacle. "Send to port six Jack."
"Okay, what is it, a service bot?" Jack selected a few icons on his screen.
"Yeah a bit more advanced than that, aren't you Sniffer?"
"Oh how cute! Okay let's see we have no trace of Jason Gilga's DNA, but we have plenty of Thoth's DNA so if the two are one and the same..." Jack sent more data to Sniffer.
"Awaiting command." Sniffer's little squeaky voice prompted, as it glided up from the receptacle.
"Oh okay then. Sniffer find Thoth, fetch there's a boy go get..."
"Tracking Sir." Sniffer shot across the lab darting from one relic to another until all samples had been indicated by a brief beam of red light.
"Well done, give him a treat." Caron crossed the lab, holding up the quill, waving its feather while giving Jack a sideways glance.
"Sniffer, find Thoth outside of this lab." Jack, shook his head at Caron "Creepy."
"Tracking." Sniffer shot out of the lab, hovered in a corridor for a moment and then began darting in and out of rooms flying just below ceiling height.
"Feisty little fella ain't he." Jack commented, watching the droid whizzing around.
"Wow!" Caron ducked as it shot over their heads.
"Well I'll leave you to it, matters demand my attention on the Bridge," Lukas wandered off.
"Yeah... Okay" Jack wasn't paying too much attention to anything other than keeping up with Sniffer, who now shot down a gravity well.
"I don't like these things," Caron hesitated at an alcove halfway along a corridor, looking down.
"Come on," Jack grabbed her hand stepping into the hole.

Caron preferred the security of throwing her arms around Jack as they floated down, stepping out at the next deck. They looked left and right, but it was Monique yelling at Sniffer which gave away its location. Caron and Jack began running toward the medical centre, only to be stopped in their tracks by a droid flashing passed them in the opposite direction.

"Your puppy needs training." Caron commented as they stopped, having lost track of Sniffer again.
"There he is." Jack set off again as doors at the far end of a passage opened and closed.
"Wot wong weh that stupid…" Yun stepped out of her quarters.
"Searching for something." Caron replied running passed. "Wong way" she further informed the puzzled Yun as they ran back, toward the gravity well.
"Clazy people." Yun shook her head, stepping back into her room.
"Oh no you don't," Caron leapt on Jack's back before he stepped into the gravity well.
"Where's it gone now?" he looked from side to side, stepping onto deck two with Caron peering over his shoulder, her legs clasping his waist.
"There," Caron pointed to a bald confused man standing outside a red hatch "Gee up Neddy" her heals tapped Jack's thighs, his arms tucked under her thighs.
"I better get a sugar lump for this." Jack trotted awkwardly, Caron bobbing up and down on his back. "Excuse me Sir have you seen a droid?"

Stephan simply pointed to the room behind him, offering a look of 'what asylum did you escape from?' Caron dismounted her steed, they entered a room full of small lights, gauges, meters. Sniffer hovered in front of a large floor to ceiling metal cylinder.

"What is that?" Jack asked Stephan.
"Perhaps you could first tell me who you are and what you're doing here?" Stephan raised eyebrows of a wrinkled face; deepening grooves in his forehead.
"Oh, er, Caron Foster, Jack Dempsey, Caron is an archaeologist I…."
"Ah yes, yes, and you're here for?"
"Tracing a DNA sample, or at least, Sniffer is." Jack pointed to the little droid.
"Most unusual, well that is, or was the ships brain."
"So that pretty much ties those threads together." Caron raised a fine eyebrow.

"Yep, Jason Gilga was Thoth!"

"Jason Gilga, is who you are looking for?" Stephan looked a little surprised.

"Ya, ever heard of him?" Jack circled the cylinder, gazing up at it.

"Indeed I worked with him briefly."

"REALLY! What was he like?" Caron's eyes widened.

"I'm not sure anyone could tell you that Miss Foster." Stephen paused for thought "He rarely conversed with anyone, I worked on the technological side of things," he pointed to lights and gauges surrounding the cylinder "while his work focused on biotechnology, the brain. Jason had a way about him, I…" Stephen slowly shook his head.

"Bit god like was he?" Jack nudged Caron.

"Ha, one would think so, it was almost a sense of fear he invoked, but not… I can't really explain it, but when he looked at you, should you be so fortunate to gain his attention, he looked straight through you."

"Yes." Caron looked distant; something that didn't escape Jack's attention.

"Yet whenever Jason was present, calmness fell over us. I wasn't conscious of it at the time, but looking back years later such things became more apparent." Stephen nodded and smiled "It was the kind of atmosphere you might expect when a holy man is present. nobody lost their temper, no bad language if something went wrong."

"Intriguing, did he ever say anything to you?" Jack appeared deep in thought.

"Not to me directly. Toward the end of our work on the last ship I think we were all on edge. We couldn't say anything to our families, didn't even know where we were working. Breeding grounds for conjecture about the military and corporations, what were we part of? Jason never got involved in any discussion, but said something once which struck a philosophical note."

"What?" Caron listened intently.

"He said that not even the mightiest wind can determine where a feather shall fall." Stephen gazed at them for a moment "Yes it provoked silence then as well."

--*--

"Some unusual readings from one planet Captain," Yoto informed Lukas as the Captain entered the Bridge.

"How so?" Lukas was glad to relax in his command seat and see that controls were finally restored.

"We expected to find the usual gas and ice planets, but not this." Mike zoomed the main screen in on a world with clouds, oceans and land masses.

"Oh there is life on Sirius, well from these here parts anyway!" Lukas gave Mike a sideways glance as if to say 'wrong again.'

"Well sentient life remains to be seen, at least inhabiting this world, but it's certainly been paid a visit." Mike felt reluctant to reveal too much, not wanting to be on the 'wrong side' again.

"Found something?"

"We'll know in a few hours, too far out yet. However the grid is showing some odd readings, we have the standard magnetic field you would expect from a life baring planet, with polar caps, atmosphere and so on, but sensors are picking up more than usual atmospheric deflection. Given this worlds distance from the A type star it shouldn't be anything more than a barren rock."

"So it has an odd atmosphere like Ashari, so what!?" Lukas shrugged.

"What is that I think these conditions are artificially generated," Mike revealed sooner than he would have liked to.

"What makes you think that?"

"Difficult to explain, could just be conditions we haven't encountered before, but spectral analysis doesn't add up either, not to mention this system isn't old enough for this world to have evolved an atmosphere such as this. At best you might expect a violent volcanic, steaming, stormy hell hole, not this gem." Mike scratched his head nervously.

"Launch a probe let's see if something shoots it down if nothing else. Wake me up if Argo is about to be eaten by a giant space frogs or something, otherwise I don't want to be disturbed, it's been a long day." Lukas stood up to leave "Well done people nice job." He gazed around the almost functional Bridge.

"Sir?" Mike's tone resonated 'where angels fear to tread' a few hours later.

"Is it green?" Lukas opened one eye, which was immediately offended by light from a console.
"Err, no sir, we…"
"Is it large?"
"Yes sir, they…"
"Is it frog like?"
"No Sir its pyramid like."
"Is it moving on an intercept course at high velocity?"
"No Sir, but…"
"Then shut the hell up and get some sleep." Lukas turned over.
"Yes Sir." Mike sighed "Damn pyramids and he wants to sleep." he muttered.

--*--

Caron's arms embraced Boggit as she slept, his nose nuzzling her cheek. Boggit's armor was perhaps her security blanket, his soft touch certainly brought comfort. Caron's dreams were filled with memories that couldn't be her own; of life during glorious times of those places she'd visited and studied ruins of. Wishful thinking no doubt, yet part of Caron wished a Prince would awaken her from what seemed like an eternal sleep. He haunted her dreams, yet in no place or time would the Prince kiss her from sleep.

"Uhh, what time is it?" She mumbled still half asleep.
"It's six AM" The console informed.
"Uck, turn the lights off, too early." An arm shot out from beneath sheets, pulling them over her head.
"Your presence is required Miss Foster." The console insisted.
"OH BOG OFF. No I wasn't talking to you Boggit, sorry. Oh well we better get up I guess." Caron rolled over, with Boggit now sitting on her hips she gifted a smile "So what are you going to do today Boggit?"
"I'm going space hopping." Boggit bounced up and down, the fluffy armadillo sounding suspiciously like a high pitched Caron.
"Morning Caron are you up and about?" Jack's voice resonated from the collar of her suit.
"Well I'm going space hopping too."
"Excuse me?" Jack gave his com controls a bewildered glance.

"Err nothing, give me five minutes Jack." Caron wondered if she even needed that what with being fully dressed an all and no need to wash, no bathroom requirements; good as there was no bathroom. "Erm." she mentally ticked off boxes "AH HA!" Caron grabbed a hair brush before anything could do it for her.

"I haven't finished my coffee yet." Lukas gave Mike the eye of death gaze across an officer's mess hall table.
"Can I get you anything then?" Mike fidgeted, filled with news that he'd already waited half the night to share.
"The usual."
"Dead pig and chicken droppings?"
"Yes ham and eggs will be fine. Ah we are honored with grace and beauty, how are you this fine morning?" Lukas smiled at Caron.
"Fine." Jack replied. "Can I get you anything Caron?"
"Dippy eggs please. Oh and lots of soldiers."
""Dippy eggs and soldiers…" Jack leant on the table with both hands, staring at Mike's empty coffee cup as if it would explain this mystery to him. "I'm sure we can find you some dippy soldiers, but erm, sorry you've lost me there."
"American's you're so uncultured." Caron laid on a heavy British upper class accent "Soft boiled eggs and fingers of bread for dipping in the egg see." She motioned up and down with a finger.
"Dippy soldiers and eggs it is then," Jack wandered over to the simulator Mike was returning from.

Lukas waited for Jack to return before finishing his coffee; he enjoyed keeping the fidgety Mike waiting. The man appeared to be shaking with excitement as he ate toast. Mike looked as if he'd had no sleep, but then he always looked that way, stress aged more than the many years of his life.

"Mike has something to announce," Lukas put down his mug, picking up a knife and fork.
"Oh, who's the lucky lady?" Caron raised a knife ominously
"WITCHA!" with one practiced swish she lopped off her egg's top, a dribble of yellow yoke signified the death of yet another innocent oval victim.
"Ya…" Mike was distracted by the insane savagery, or was it the

savage insanity, he couldn't quite decide.

"Ohh Monique isn't it? You ol devil you!" Lukas gestured at Mike with a fork.

"I should be so lucky." Mike sighed.

"Mmm Yummy" a soldier met it's fate, covered in yoke entering the mouth of doom, between deep red lips, white teeth cut it in half.

"Oh please!" Mike shook his head, ripping eyes away from yokey lust. "Ahem, right, we are orbiting a planet, which to my great surprise is teaming with life. Tectonically stable, breathable atmosphere, seems too good to be true really."

"Awesome." Jack sat back from his hash browns.

"Yes and more, we have evidence of the artificial nature of things here, as I mentioned last night Lukas."

"You did indeed."

"Pyramids at the poles are…"

"PYRAMIDS!" a soldier drowned in an eggy pool as yolk dribbled down sides of Caron's breakfast. "When, I, are we..?"

"Yes pyramids, they are transmitting… well we're not sure yet, but its influencing the planets electromagnetic field. We also suspect they are creating some form of shield through the thermo and mesosphere's protecting this planet from solar influences, meteors and…"

"Giant space frogs? A little less science and a little more sense Mike if you will."

"Right, err, life forms we have detected so far are predominantly reptilian, advanced in the evolutionary scheme of things. In other words this world has been terraformed."

"So we are dealing with sentient life forms?" Lukas stiffened.

"Doubtful, there are other testaments to advanced influence, but these are ruins, pyramids, possibly temples, monoliths and the like, but no cities, roads and such."

"Visited then, but why build such things if there is no sentient life to appreciate it?" Jack commented.

"Good point." Mike shrugged.

"Well the ancients kept telling us, I mean they might as well have left a travel brochure recommending some hotels and excursions!" Caron was dizzy with anticipation.

"Any insight from the twins?" Lukas felt sure no mystery was to

mystifying for the mysterious pair.
"No oddly they can't pick up on anything, possibly the shielding I mentioned, our sensors are relaying only a fraction of what they should do." Mike frowned.
"Can't say this sits too well with me Mike," Lukas crossed his arms.
"We can't come all this way and not go down there." Caron wished she knew how to pilot a shuttle.
"Ya, obviously, but you Miss Foster will need to rein it in, be patient, you and Jack need to train with various equipment before we go down there." Lukas gave a stern glare, not wanting to deal with any further drama from her past.
"Okay, guess I have no choice in the matter." Caron dreaded facing her technological fears.
"No I'm afraid you don't. There are repairs to complete before we can even launch a shuttle anyway, so make good use of the next day or so." Lukas returned attention to his meal.
"Actually we have managed to retrieve shuttle three, it's in the main bay now." Mike waited for a reprimand.
"Really? That still leaves the hanger door to deal with."
"Yes, with your leave we need to launch two interceptors, with adapted weapons we believe it's possible to heat the upper door and bring it back in alignment. Gearing should take a matter of hours to replace."
"Okay. You have been busy Mike, well done. Set things in motion and then get some rest, stop jacking up on the stimulants you look like a wreck waiting to happen."
"Yes, Sir, the operations need careful supervision though and…."
"Monique."
"Yes Luke."
"I want Mike Palmer confined to the medical centre until…"
"Okay, okay I'll de-stimulate, just give me a few hours." Mike held up his hands, surrendering to the Captain's demands which he considered more reasonable that Monique lecturing about stimulant abuse.
"Belay that Monique."
"Oh I dunno, you might get lucky there Mike, Doctors an nurses an all." Jack grinned.
"Ahem, well, I had better set things in motion. Captain." Mike

nodded and left before trouble could find him.

Caron endured her training, though she questioned the necessity of knowing how to fire weapons, continually pointed out that this was all pointless as she would never do this and that and the majority of it could go to hell as far as she was concerned. CAP units were eventually classified as 'fun' due to terrorizing others with her flying antics. Jack soothed her nerves every step of the way, kneeling by Caron's side, trying to give some comfort after the ordeal of learning about virtual vision behind a dark visor. She hyperventilated the first time, gradually getting used to feeling that being held in the dark was okay. Naming her suit 'Binky', promptly followed by 'night vision' whenever the dark visor activated brought an end to the panic attacks. By lunchtime Caron was a self proclaimed Thunder CAP warrior, not a bird, not a plane, no just a flying menace.

"You'll sleep well tonight." Mike grinned at Caron and Jack across the mess hall table.
"Nearly fell asleep during the briefing." Caron yawned "No offence, but tactical landing zones and air support just isn't my thing."
"You done with that?" Jack enquired of her tuna casserole.
"Yeah I'm stuffed, breakfast, lunch AND dinner, geesshh, I get fat eating rabbit food."
"Yep well you burnt up your soldiers this morning at least." Jack tucked into remains of tuna casserole. "Want to watch a movie this evening?" Jack summoned courage to take a step not taken since the death of his wife.
"Oh… yeah that would…" Caron stifled an 'OH my God did he really say that?'
"Your presence might be required this evening" Mike fiddled with a hypo spray "Chin up." he leant over pressing the device against Jack's neck releasing a hiss. "That will keep you awake. Caron."
"Oh more thrilling talk about what we're not doing?" Caron's eyes rolled.
"Alpha group report to hanger deck immediately" Yoto's command echoed around the ship.
"What's going..?" Caron wondered at marines and pilots

scrambling out of the mess hall while others continued conversations.

"Well if you had been listening to the briefing you would know that's you guys," Mike gestured to the hatch "Step it up."

Chapter Six: One small step for man, one giant..?

"A few updates on our mission briefing. Air drop is a negative, there are numerous flying… things above the forest canopy. Our alpha Oscar is…" Lukas addressed Alpha group assembled before shuttle one; nicknamed Huntress.
"At our what?" Caron nudged Jack.
"Mission area," Jack whispered back.
"… three clicks South, close to the valley entrance, the closest LZ to our pyramid.
"What.?"
"Landing Zone."
"Oooohhh."
"Alpha One will be traveling on foot, or caping through deep forestation, Alpha Two will take samples at LZ and follow as study dictates. Play it by ear people, there are many unknowns down there. I want to make one thing very clear and that is your conduct during our little trip." Griffin paced from left to right. "We will no doubt encounter various critters, some of which are on the gigantic side of large, others, well we don't have a whole lot of intel, BUT I do NOT want the human race to announce it's arrival by blasting everything in sight, IS THAT CLEAR."
"Yes Sir," military personnel replied in unison, leaving Caron wondering if she should have said something in the affirmative department, but no, she was sure no one noticed.
"You don't have to salute," Jack also reminded Caron, whose hand hovered around her forehead.
"Your weapons are preset to emit an electric charge, hopefully enough to warn off any civilian eating set of mobile jaws. IF, and only IF life is endangered are you to kill anything, so keep your damn fingers off those triggers. Okay let's get to it." With that said, Lukas boarded shuttle one.

Caron sat nervously, harnessed into a seat with Jack on one side, Arten and Dharma on another; occupying one row of seats. Before them the forward wall became a screen displaying large doors opening. Huntress began to glide into the launch bay, triggering warning sirens, alerting any deranged stoner to get out of the hanger bay; doing nothing to ease Caron's nerves.

"Oww, I dunno if I want to look." Ominous outer doors opened to the abyss of space.
"My father often spoke of you Miss Foster." Anwar, sitting behind, leant forward taking an opportunity to speak to, and distract Caron.
"Your Father? Who was he?"
"Rakin, Rakin Nassar, he was a guide when we lived in Cairo."
"Oh…" Caron accessed memory banks, dismissing various images from her mind of being blown to bits, either by the vacuum of space or some horrific explosive accident. "Oh yes I remember, he had a delightful way of describing the gods, not that I'm sure they would have approved!"
"Yes he told many funny stories, I never tired of hearing them." Anwar smiled at the memories. "Do you remember me?"
"Not the skinny little runaway who was always in trouble!?"
"Yes that was me." Anwar laughed "He put a dog leash on me once."
"What a small world!" Caron was now oblivious to Huntress gently gliding forward and out clearing the bay.

Gracefully the hawk's wings splayed out on either side. Wings locked in place, an electric blue light blazed across engine ports, blasting Huntress away from Argo at phenomenal speeds. Pilot Grant and navigator Rhianna testing systems before attempting descent to the planet that rapidly became a speck behind them.

"She seems fine Captain," Grant gazed over cockpit instruments, nodding at Rhianna sitting to his right; monitoring navigation amongst other functions. "Starting approach."
"Take it easy, can't tell what reactions we may provoke," Lukas, sitting in a row adjacent to civilian crew members, reminded the often over confident pilot.
"Yes Sir," Grant wondered how many times he'd heard that.
"So magical," Caron eyes glazed as Huntress came about and approached a radiant sphere of life. "Our souls dwell unseen within us, worlds hide their souls in plain sight for only Heavens to see."

Sphere soon became crescent as the hawk began entering upper atmosphere. Jack delighted in his suit's protective properties, if it were not for this, Caron would have drawn blood by now as her hand clasped his leg. She wasn't the only one experiencing a few frayed nerves from the shuttle's increasingly violent shuddering. This wasn't at all usual.

"Report. Grant."
"No problem Captain, It'll be rough for a minute or so," Grant replied from the head of a flaming bird, gazing over at Rhianna.
"Altering vector, slow it down Grant." Rhianna's shaky hands danced over controls.
"She's surfing, just can't penetrate upper atmosphere."
"Oh crap," Caron's free hand grasped her seat, reacting to helmet deployment.
"Perfectly normal," Jack lied. "Haven't you been on a shuttle before?"
"YES."
"Oh."
"Sorry about this guys, nearly through," Grant also lied.
"What are you two planning?" Lukas eyed the twins suspiciously, noticing a look between them; a sign they were talking to each other in ways only their kind had learnt or evolved to.
"We are not attractive," their thoughts were offered to the Captain.
"What do you mean?" Lukas frowned, questioning the twin's mental state.
"Attraction and repulsion, fundamental laws of…" Arten began to explain.
"Ohhh!" Lukas smiled at a penny dropping. "Grant, activate landing polarity."
"Wha… which Sir?"
"Try one and then the…" Lukas paused, as Arten answered, "Positive, try positive."
"Okay Sir," Grant shrugged at Rhianna who mouthed 'WHAT!?'

Suddenly the hawk dropped like a stone. Although this brought panic to the helm, Arten returned the Captain's smile. Momentarily plummeting, Grant slammed on thrusters, breaking the sound barrier more times than advisable, booming into darkness, moon replaced Sun. Gradually Huntress returned to a graceful flight through clouds, while Rhianna tried to figure out where they were after a carefully calculated flight plan had just been thrown out of the window.

"That way," Rhianna pointed across Grant to the left.
"Sorry that's a bit too technical for me; have to look that one up when I get back," he raised eyebrows at Rhianna.
"Just point it over there while I figure details shmuck."
"If you say so. Good morning everybody!" Daylight returned. Grant took Huntress down to take a look, cruising a few hundred feet above a sparkling ocean.
"Wow, Awesome," and other such exclamations spread amongst the crew, provoked by a huge mountain standing alone, rising from a deep ocean and shrouded with clouds.
"That's enough for my retirement fund! I claim this rock in the name of Wayne Rushden."
"That's gotta be at least a zillion tons, of gold. Maggie underestimated a vein streaking through the mountain as if it were a golden lightening bolt.
"Yep and where there's gold there's…" Tyler's eyes widened.
"DRAGON!" Rhianna almost deafened a mesmerized Grant.
"That vein must be half a mile wide, uhhhh." Jack grabbed his seat instinctively, the ship banked sharply to avoid a collision.
"… dragons!" Tyler informed everyone, although they had all reached similar conclusions.
"It's a flying reptile, a big one I admit, massive wing span on that thing. But I'm sure it doesn't kidnap maidens and duel with knights." Lukas tried to calm chatter. "Grant watch your speed, what's our ETA?"
"Twelve minutes Sir, at this speed." Grant's watched the horizon intently "That's if Twinkie here hasn't got the map upside down again."
"Oh spin on it," Rhianna offered a finger.
"Ya later, just watch for anything big in tha air will ya."
"Approaching land mass, multiple targets… flying things, to be avoided I mean." Rhianna's eyes darted from instruments to sky and back again.

"Hey nice beach man. Captain can we…"
"No!"
"Ahh surely we got some shore leave due?"
"Let's find out what might have you for a barbeque first eh Wayne."
"Damn I didn't bring my shorts." Caron melted at the thought of running across that sand, diving in the ocean, building sand castles and watching hot…
"Oh I'm sure we can simulate something suitable," Jack's imagination brought a grin to his face, which soon fell to a stern look from Dharma.
"Atmosphere confirmed sixty nine percent nitrogen, thirty percent oxygen, acceptable trace elements. That's stink to you guys." Rhianna informed the crew "Local time is dawn-ish, we hope you had a pleasant flight, now get off."

Creatures took to wings, multiple legs or claws at the sight of this new and formidable predator descending. It's two legs furnishing massive claws emerging between wings and belly. Ferns crushed in a perfect circle under influence of opposing magnetic forces; Huntress matching ground polarity, cushioning the hawks landing. Stanchions hissed bearing weigh, stabilizing 'claws' sinking into earthy ground before a final hiss from stanchion legs, lowering the belly to ground level. A dozen marines burst forth into flattened ferns and grass shaded by a wing. Baring pulse rifles sweeping air from side to side, guards fanned out to form a perimeter.

"Area secure Sir." Anwar gazed up, ready to slay any dragon that might regard him as a tooth pick.
"Real air!" Caron spun around with arms out as helmets retracted and crew assembled at the edge of a clearing in what could barely be called a semi tropical forest, offering little more than grasses, ferns and palms the size of giant redwood trees rising out of mist, reaching hundreds of feet high.
"Okay, Alpha Two set up by that outcrop of rocks, they should provide some cover while you poke around with your gizmo's.
"Lukas pointed to eastern smooth boulders "Keep a sharp eye Anwar, our landing probably scared off everything, but I'm sure that won't last for long. When you're done there take the eastern

ridge toward our Target Zone. Alpha One, travel light, leave those rifles here. No," the Captain waved his hand down noticing Wayne and Tyler swinging CAP control arms down to their waists "lets stretch our legs for a while." he led the way winding through undergrowth.
"Looks like something's headed in the same direction as us Lukas," Jack knelt by a large indentation hewn into the soil "large biped moving at high speed judging by the distance between these prints and the dirt thrown up. Big claws too! There's barely six inches of soil here Captain, then its sand. If it wasn't for the size of these palms I'd say this area was underwater not so long ago." he looked up at Lukas, holding a handful of sandy dirt.
"As Mike said this world has probably been terraformed, icecaps may have been forming over the passed few thousand years lowering sea levels, there's a lot of islands with sparse vegetation. Let Alpha Two worry about all the science," Lukas shrugged.

Sound returned to the valley as Alpha One cautiously followed a dried up river bed, earth had replaced water and the forest became thicker. Strange plants tempted investigation, their beautiful vibrant colors being the last thing many little armored creatures ever saw. An almost invisible war waged between plant and insect life, tendrils wrapped around a beetle that fought back with pincers in a duel to the death. Many eyes observed the alien invaders, while tentacles felt the vibration of their movement or caught what little scent these beings gave off. For the most part these intruders were too large to be worthy of any attention, though some creatures had eyes bigger than their bellies and fangs to match.

"What's that?" Tyler looked up sharply for a source of ear piercing screeching.
"There," Maggie drew her sidearm almost as fast as helmets reacted to rapid movement coming their way.
"Gesshh!" Wayne ducked, others threw themselves to the ground as a flying blur with claws took a swipe at him.
"Nother," Maggie fired hitting the first black winged, rat sized reptile that's claws and fangs would seem better fitted to a larger creature.
"Get the.." Tyler stumbled around as another clawed at his back,

trying to latch on with fine claws without much success, its leathery wings beating frantically.

"Gah gnnn." Arten seemed to growl moving more swiftly that eyes could follow, a sparkling glint snatched the writhing, screeching lizard, it's blood spraying across Tyler's back barely a second before parts of it lay in a mangled heap.

"Shhh" Dharma threw her arms around Arten, who turned his back on others as if trying to hide something.

"You okay kid?" Lukas halted his approach, met by Dharma's glaring eyes warning him off.

"He'll be okay. Violence is not good for him Mr Lukas." Dharma excused, still calming her brother.

"I think its deceased there Tyler!" Lukas frowned at the marine stomping on its carcass "And I don't think we want that one trying its luck again." A red pulse of light shot from his sidearm, frying the first offender.

"Think we oughta get a refund from that travel agent," Wayne glanced at a motion detector, multiple blue dots moving randomly within a one click radius came as no surprise.

"Reeaalll primitive," Tyler couldn't put his eyes in enough places at the same time, trying not to trip over rocks while watching tree tops.

"Feels like we've gone back in time a few hundred million years when reptiles ruled the Earth," Caron avoided stepping on an insect that couldn't decide which way to run.

"Place gives me tha creeps," Tyler gawped at vines sliding around a tree trunk.

"Ya, I think we're being sized up." Maggie's hand hovered near her weapon, "Two O'clock."

"It's a salad muncher," Caron noted vegetation hanging from the creatures mouth.

"Looks like a giant spiky tortoise." Wayne wondered how anything could attack it without being impaled on ivory thorns.

"If nothing else it means there's no large predators in the vicinity." Jack laid on a good measure of wishful thinking.

"It's got," Caron cautiously moved closer, the creature's head following her movement nervously, "vines or something around its neck."

"Yep well I don't think taking it for a ride is on the agenda, c'mon

lets move on," Lukas signaled.
"Sir!" Maggie began moving toward the giant tortoise.
"Oh crap, hey over here guys no playing with the monsters," Lukas called to Dharma and Arten who hovered by it, stroking the creatures nose. "Maggie I told you to keep an eye on them, CARON, get back here… Oh Aunt Grief."

After virtually everyone adopting a giant pet, the party moved on, distracted by so much. Huge plants impersonating obese pineapples sat amidst ferns, palm tree sentinels now shared sunlight with what appeared to be fungus columns, as if someone had chopped thousands of red fly agaric mushrooms in half and stuck them to a tree trunk. Grotesque beak shaped noses served as branches, hairy tentacles dangling from nostrils gathered pollen. Bright orange flower heads never blossomed, instead making whooping whispers when suddenly opening to capture flying insects.

"Jenson will be having orgasms about this lot, probably have to leave those guys here for a thousand years or force them back to the ship at gunpoint!" Lukas waited for Caron and Jack to catch up. "What you grinning at mischief?" he noted Dharma smiling at Caron and Jack holding hands, chatting away while navigating around boulders.
"Butterflies." she cryptically responded, though Arten rolled his eyes at her fluttering girlie thoughts. "Not the only ones are they," she poked a tongue at Arten. "Secret butterflies." Dharma teased flapping her arms gracefully.
"I don't…" Arten's eyes glared at his sister.
"Yummy Yun…"
"Alright, enough," Lukas really didn't want to witness two psychics squabbling.
"Kartha butterflies too!" Dharma grinned at Lukas as she wandered on arms out to her sides rising and falling gently.
"WHAT?" Lukas looked distinctly guilty.
"Oh so Kartha is it?" Tyler put a hand to his heart and fluttered eyelashes at him.

An hours trek brought the group toward a small clearing. There another creature stopped Alpha One in its tracks, small, but curious in that it appeared to be carrying fruit of some kind. Lukas signaled for everyone to keep low, wishing to observe the reptilian biped that stood about three feet high. It scavenged around the base of a tree searching for bluish round fruit.

"It's a chameleon, can hardly see it now." Maggie shielded her eyes from sunlight, straining to see the creature that's coloring had become that of the tree.
"Is that gold shimmering around it's neck, it's wearing jewelry! Intelligence, civility even!" Jack's excitement made it hard to keep his voice down.
"This is humanities first encounter with alien intelligence… well at least officially." Caron's face beamed with the magnitude of this.
"Lets not jump to conclusions, it doesn't look civil enough to build pyramids, might have even found that jewelry, or been given it by those who did build here. We should wait for Alpha Two to make contact, Jenson and Natasha would want to do their botanical, biological, palaeontological, psychopathic, ecology mumbo jumbo." Lukas twirled his hands again.
"Stuff," Caron suggested.
"Yeah that's the one."
"Aww, come on, where there's one there could be many, better that we say hi now rather than run into a whole tribe of them and cause panic or worse. This one's isolated, we can make friends without a face off."
"Let's just observe for now Caron," Lukas whispered.
"I feel that she's feminine Mr Lukas," Dharma peeked over the Captain's shoulder.
"Young, intelligent but not intellectual," Arten added.
"Natasha," Lukas activated his helmet, transmitting what he could see to the paleontologist, "What do you make of this?"
"Ahh, your not coming through too well Mr. Griffin."
"It's a chameleon, not too easy to see."
"Transmission is fuzzy."
"Oh great, well reptilian biped, three feet high, tail about that too, skull shape, err a bit like a German Shepherd dog, no ears that I can see, almost human like arms."
"Teeth, claws, spines?"

"Can't see any from here, its head is, well more smooth than a dogs, dog meets bird in collision with lizard kinda deal."
"Ya, I can see it a bit clearer now, similar to a velociraptor but without wings. If it's of that family give it a wide birth Captain, raptors are fast moving lethal predators."
"Okay, how's it going with Alpha Two?"
"I, it's just paradise here, barely know where to begin, we…"
"Good, good well gotta push on here, thanks Natasha." Lukas retracted the helmet rather than listen to endless scientific observations. "You get that?"
"Yeah can't base life here on what little we know of Earth prehistory though." Jack shrugged off comparisons "Have they ever found fossils wearing jewelry?"
"True," Lukas tried to weigh things up and make a decision.

Caron couldn't take her eyes off the little reptile. In some respects she resembled vicious raptors of Earth's prehistoric era, yet she was strangely soft in appearance with smooth facial scales. Its eyes conveyed a sense of gentleness, their slender line flowing into flaps **to** either side of her head; like elongated eyelids, twitching at any sound. The creature walked upright in an almost human fashion, except for a slight stoop, no doubt caused by a prominent tail. Her arms now holding three or four of the blue coconut sized fruits, she detected unfamiliar smells, gazing nervously in Alpha One's direction before turning to head back toward western forestation.

"Settles that then, give it a minute and we'll move on, let Alpha… Caron!" Lukas tried to grab her, too late, she walked slowly toward the reptile.
"Umm, hi there," Caron knew full well the creature wouldn't speak English, but Boggit always understood her… sort of. "Oh, oh it's okay, don't be scared," Caron crouched slightly trying not to seem such a threat in response to the reptiles shrill screech, plainly terrified, dropping fruit and freezing, visibly trembling.
"Nnn, nu, nunan, nunan" Throwing itself to the ground, face in the dirt, she stretched arms toward Caron.
"Sir we have activity to the West, multiple targets, scattered, about twelve moving this way," Tyler alerted.

"More like that one I would imagine, ETA?"
"Ten minutes maybe more, moving fast but erratic."
"Okay, hold your ground." Lukas gestured for them to stay low.
"Hey, I'm not gonna hurt you." Caron picked up one of the fruits that had rolled her way, but the creatures face was firmly planted, fearing to even look up, its color now that of grass.
"Nunan, nunan."
"Erm, I am Caron, Caron, you?" she cautiously reached out, touching a webbed, scaly hand, tipped with four white nails, one to the side of others, "She has opposable thumbs Jack."
"And no doubt enough intelligence to make tools… and weapons." Jack thought aloud acknowledging the significance of opposable thumbs.
"I won't hurt you," Caron moved closer trying to gently lift the reptiles head, "Oh, err…" Caron flinched a little in response to ear flaps twitching "Sorry must be ticklish eh?"
"Kicchhh" she hissed briefly looking up at Caron and then over her shoulder.
"Yes, erm whatever, hey, sit, sit with me, you." She pointed at the reptile and then at her own butt on the ground "Oh crap" Caron's heard a familiar 'Screeee' and tried to cover her head with hands that hit a faster reacting helmet.
"KAH" much like a cat extending claws, nails turned into three inch talons as the creature hurled ten feet into the air, a blur of fangs and claws, snatching the winged menace in mid flight, prompting Dharma to share a surprised exchange of thoughts with Arten.
"Thank you," Caron blinked at the mangled item now being offered to her by a cowering reptile.
"Ech nunan," she laid the dead predator in front of Caron.
"Remind me not to make rude remarks about the natives!" Wayne holstered his weapon again.
"Me Caron, you?" Caron managed to convince the still frightened being to sit with her, gesturing back and forth.
"Nunan," her inner eyelids blinked.
"No nunan, CA RON, me, KA-RON, you?" Caron hoped her name didn't mean 'I'm going to rip your head off and where's the nearest spaceport please.'
"Krun, Kahrun."

"YES yes that's it… sort of! You?"
"Sshhhhssteecchh." The reptiles heart pounded.
"Ohhh… Shtech, well that's a nice name, umm, DAAR-MA, DAR-MA" Caron pointed to the forest, waving in a beckoning manner.
"Shood, dach." Shtech pointed to the West and then herself, trembling as Dharma approached "Nnn nunan." She almost melted under a blue eyed gaze.
"Human, you mean HU MAN!?"
"Uiche nunan" Shtech pointed at both Caron and Dharma, who now knelt and soothed the reptile "Gach dol?" she pointed to the Sun.
"Yes, from up there," Caron pointed to herself then sky.
"Chhan, chhan shood dach," Shtech stood up pointing to the West taking Caron and Dharma's hands in her own.
"Oh, okay, erm, Shtech, nunun, erm more, more" Caron gestured Southward, where gradually more of Alpha One emerged.
"Gad nuuuunan!" Shtech's trembling turned from fear to that of wonder and excitement, yes siree she would be the chief okal of the pond when she arrived with this batch of prophecy fruit.
"Yes, lot's of nunan's! We go see." Caron prompted her to continue.
"Oishna?" Shtech glared at Lukas who'd picked up a blue fruit.
"Yum, taste good?" Lukas brought the fruit to his mouth.
"Nunan, uldch!" Her head tilted to one side, blinking inner eyelids; puzzled by such bizarre behavior.

Faced with what lay before it and what chased behind, the Gughru thundered passed Alpha One offering a wonderful impression of a miniature triceratops as it done so. It wasn't long before they heard undergrowth being trampled underfoot ahead and others of Shtech's kind calling her name. The words 'Nunan gach dol hoocchhki KULDA' virtually silenced the forest and Shtech seemed very proud of her little self. Spear carrying reptiles stopped and looked at each other, not quite knowing what to do. They moved forward cautiously and then, as if hitting a wall, threw themselves to the ground chanting 'Nunan, nunan.' A few further away made a run for it, calling 'nunan' as they ran toward hillside caves.

Panic incited chaos in a deep system of caves as word spread, the word being 'nunan' until reptiles dressed in green, adorned with jewelry of gold and gems, began calming things down and giving orders for the gathering of fruits, precious stones and anything else they could think of to appease the gods.

"So err Jack, going back to the divine nature of the Argo crew," Caron wore a broad grin.
"Yeah, yeah you just have to be right, don't you? Well you have your parade, oh goddess of the scaly ones."
"Here comes the King," Lukas presumed of a reptile in green robes, who approached and bowed deeply.
"Come, plee, please, old one speak," the elderly reptile bowed continuously.
"You speak English!?" Lukas wasn't alone in shock.
"I would say it's a given that Thoth had influence amongst these people, we already know he was here?" Jack reminded the Captain.
"Of course, yes that makes sense," Lukas breathed easier with a dose of logic.
"These elders probably know more of our language." Caron tired of constant chanting, which grew louder as they climbed the well trodden path toward a large cave entrance. "Arten could you do something to stop the god worship?"
"Yes Miss Caron." he closed eyes.
"Telepathic influence guys." Lukas managed to say before their minds filled with images and feelings of serenity, standing tall, friendship and mutual respect.
"Hichinrea!" Reptiles stopped chanting, instead standing up, holding their heads in wonder, awestruck that 'nunan' gods had filled their heads with visions and feelings.
"Anyone know what the hell this thing is on my leg, because I want it OFF!" Maggie tried not to look at the green monkey like reptile clinging to her thigh.
"Well goddess it looks harmless but you have subjects to command, ask them." Lukas suggested, gesturing to rows of reptiles standing like an honor guard either side of the path and further anxious eyes watching them from forest cover.
"You," Maggie pointed to a tall muscular warrior standing over

five feet. "Get this off." She pointed at the almost smooth skinned critter that had taken a liking to her.

The anxious warrior approached wondering if he would be punished for allowing the hokuut to touch a nunan, as it was obviously not worthy of such an honor. He bowed and gently coerced the hokuut, which climbed his arm and perched on the warrior's shoulder.

"Ahh it's a little pet," Caron smiled.
"Hokuut kuut ga nerch," the warrior explained, waving a hand over forest and then to his eyes.
"HA! It's a watch frog," Lukas laughed.
"Old speak time."
"Yes let's go and speak with this old one and then continue with our mission people. Lead, yes, yes, old one." Lukas gestured to the elderly reptile to get on with it. "What is name of your… err, all of you?" he gestured with a sweep of an arm.
"We Kahkuri gather as one."
"And you, what is your name?"
"I Presht.. Priest, Ochda." The old rep hobbled along.
"I think this one is Shtech's Mother." Dharma pointed to a Kahkur female, distinguished from males by narrower eyes and a more slender neck. "Yes, come, come."

Dharma waved for the Kahkur to come closer. The female kept her distance, walking a few yards away nervously glancing from Shtech, to the priest, Dharma and warriors as if she were doing something wrong. With some help from the priest, Shmeh was persuaded to walk with them. Shtech then went to great lengths telling mother how it all was and therefore she should have more sweet fruit… much more, and definitely no achgul or dould for that matter! Shtech and her mother took familiar blue fruit from a basket as they entered caves. More female Kahkur did likewise, following them in. It soon became apparent why. Fruits glowed, lighting tunnels connecting a series of caves. Caron insisted that they stop now and then to examine wall paintings, most depicted scenes of everyday life, tributes to the exalted or battles with great beasts.

"I hope we don't run into one of those!" Tyler squinted in the glowing blue fruit light at little stick figures throwing spears toward something best described as a massive crab with attitude. "It's got a crab like body, with a long neck, thick arm pincer things." He described the monster to those not close enough to see. "Rows of nasty ass jagged teeth in its head."
"Agag!" Shtech informed Tyler, taking his hand and leading him to an alcove nearby. "Agag heth," she pointed to a tooth half her size "RRAAAARRRRR." Shtech grinned baring her own fangs.
"Yeah, BIG rrarr!" Tyler's gut churned at the thought "You see, kinda tortoise thing?" He gestured trying to visually describe the beast they'd seen, which puzzled Shtech for a while.
"Uolm?" she led Tyler to the far side of that cave being careful to guide him around floor mats, in fact their bedding.
"Yeah that's it, you ride them." The group gathered around looking at the painting of stick figures sitting on an Uolm.
"Slow, very slow?" Wayne lurched around, provoking a hooting sound from Shmeh, others soon relaxed into what was their way of laughing.
"Ingli folkmoot, goot," Shtech gave him a sideways look.

Curling into a ball on the floor, tucking arms and legs in, Shtech acted out just what an uolm could do. Slowly arms and legs unfolded from beneath her until she was spread eagled. Then suddenly Shtech raced around the cave on all fours, revealing that this wasn't so unnatural for Kahkuri, evolution still had a ways to go.
"Oh, not such a tortoise then, or maybe that's the secret of how the tortoise won that race with the hare!" Caron joined laughter at Shtech's antics.
"Yes indeed, well now we have answered the great mystery we should return home to our masters eh. C'mon people we have work to do." Lukas gestured toward the old priest someway along a tunnel.
"They sleep on fern beds and eat from golden bowls!" Maggie was somewhat awed by the amount of golden implements scattered around.
"It's probably as common to them as steel or tin is to us." Jack had

a sense of foreboding about the matter. "Perhaps we should keep such things to ourselves for their sake."

"I don't think the great corporate would want their own gold stash devalued by tons of this being shipped home anyway." Lukas leant toward Jack, talking in a hushed tone "Could easily create instability."

"Food of the gods," Caron commented, "And not in the way of material wealth either. Several ancient civilizations attributed spiritual growth to…"

"Michga, michga Churun," Shtech held the flat of her hand to Caron as they approached a distinctly rectangular doorway.

"Michga." Other Kahkuri stopped and bowed.

"Priest place, holy." The old priest pointed to the doorway.

"Younger say… you bye."

"Oh, goodbye, Michga Shtech," Caron laid a hand on Shtech's as did the rest of Alpha One before entering the doorway.

Chapter Seven: The spirit of Ra

"Blessed we are for prophecy is fulfilled."

An old priest attempted to bow, seated in a wooden chair at the far end of a chamber. Six younger priests attended, standing to his side. All around the group endless words and pictures covered smooth walls, pillars and ceiling. Large golden bowls contained juice of blue fruits providing light to simple, but precise architecture that contrasted with natural caves and roughly hewn tunnels. A hollowed, intricately carved log glistened with gems and golden jewelry set before a stone table flowing with fruits and flowers. Gifts for the honored guests that the Kahkuri had awaited for centuries.

"Greetings, I am Lukas."
"We are blessed great Lahkus, I am your servant Echraoul, keeper of words." His shaky arm gestured to a stone box that's lid had been removed in their honor.
"Oxford English Dictionary!" Caron peered in reading a book's embossed and somewhat well worn cover. "Thoth certainly has a sense of humor."
"Well Sniffer isn't reading any human or Thothy DNA." Jack examined his suit's readings.
"Who gave this to you?" Caron didn't even want to touch the book, fearing such might damage its fragile pages.
"Lord Theta of the Star." Echraoul's croaky voice incited homage from his apprentice priests.
"Gaver of words."
"Gaver of numbers."
"Gaver of time."
"Gaver of forge."
"Gaver of knowing."
"Gaver of all," the final priest bowed.
"He told our ancestors of your coming from Earth. That we must pass down sacred word from age to age," Echraoul wheezed.
"Why don't all Kahkuri speak these words?" Caron's sensibilities began to prickle.

"They are sacred, only I may touch diction."
"Hmm, maybe to preserve the book," Jack reasoned.
"Or control, power, the elite, something so familiar about this Jack and I don't like it." Caron reflected on how a few possessing knowledge while the masses were ignorant, had held back humanity for so long. "You know that if this crap hadn't happened on Earth we might have the answers to our own dilemma by now." She spoke in hushed tones to Jack while examining wall depictions.
"The dark ages and such?" Jack sought to clarify.
"Dark ages, religious wars, destruction of knowledge again and again. I think our own visitors educated humans, gave us a kick start and now the clocks run out, we screwed up!"
"Yeah, you can say that again." Wayne mumbled.
"All we have done is slaughter each other for thousands of years over WHAT? God said this or God done that, well I'm damn sure God didn't want everything destroyed over differences of opinion." Caron knew she should keep such discussions between them, but her anger ran deep.
"Okay, okay, save it for later. You have served well Echraoul, we are pleased and must study your efforts." Lukas patted Caron's shoulder, turning to the old priest deploying some diplomacy.
"They have only done what they thought was right," Jack nudged Caron.
"We are pleased and feel your wisdom is such that it must be shared amongst all Kahkuri, teach them the meaning." Caron waved at walls, "In your people's own words. This is our wish! Isn't it?" She elbowed the Captain.
"Yes, yes this is our wish, we shall gift to you more sacred diction."
"More?" Jack questioned.
"Minus the harmful stuff, more like a how to farm, build and live without screwing up the planet books."
"Ah yes thou art wise great leader, ahem." Caron smirked.
"We wish to speak with Theth, Theta I mean." Lukas addressed the elder priest.
"Theta return many time ago to Earth."
"Oh great!" Jack seemed to wither.
"Prophecy telling you speak with mountain." Echraoul pointed to

depictions on the left wall.

"The pyramid." Caron gazed at the last picture in a series, amidst thousands of words. "If peaceful heart they carry, truth shall they know, if hatred they bare guardians shall consume." She read aloud.

"Perhaps a warning to keep the natives away," Lukas speculated.

"Ya right." Caron's sarcasm spoke volumes. "Your people, do they go to the mountain?"

"No, mountain is dwelling of ancients, only star people may go there." Echraoul pointed to Lukas.

"Who built the mountain?" Jack fished for clues.

"Ancient ones, star people."

"Figures." Jack expected as much "Yes you have honored our predecessors well with you recollection." He disguised their ignorance as a test for the priests.

"Let's roll people we have a mountain to move, at least that's what it feels like." The Captain nodded to a confused Echraoul and turned to leave.

"Are gifts not pleasing!?" An apprentice seemed most disturbed at their parting without the long awaited way things are meant to happen, that had changed from generation to generation.

"Others will soon follow." Lukas announced, which appeased anxieties. "First we must speak with other star people." This definitely set things in order.

"Yes, yes your brothers, the way Murnk will show." Echraoul gestured to his son who beckoned them to follow him through a narrow opening behind Echraoul.

Blindly Murnk led the way through a natural fissure in the rock. Alpha One soon demonstrated divine powers, activating helmets and their headlights, fortunate at times when heads bumped against rock. They squeezed, crawled and clambered through secret passages that unlike many parts of their warrens, had not been hewn out by the Kahkuri. Regrets spread amongst them for taking what they had hoped would be a shortcut, but eventually Murnk stopped and would proceed no further, pointing toward daylight streaming into the passage ahead. 'Eye to mountain' Murnk had stated before bowing. Thanking Murnk, who feared to go any further, Alpha One emerged into daylight, standing on a ledge where they could see the white smooth sided pyramid from above the tree canopy, its golden cap stone brilliant, reflecting sunlight.

"That's what the great pyramid in Egypt once looked like." Caron's helmet visor darkened, shielding her eyes from glare. "Looks like it just landed there; smack in the middle of the jungle."
"For all we know, it could have Wayne." Pulling down a CAP control arm, Jack rested his left arm into it, grasping the joystick, as there seemed to be no easy way down from the ledge. "Certainly no sign of tracks, quarrying, or anything that would indicate building such a thing."
"It is pure." Dharma tried to put what she sensed into words.
"In the alchemical sense?" Caron questioned.
"As a Queen, without disgrace, wise, watching, mighty, majestic, commanding respect." Arten expounded.
"Yep it's big alright." Tyler brought things right down to Earth, or at least the unnamed world that currently provided ground zero.
"Write poetry do you Tyler?" Dharma stood with a hand on her hip, while others rolled their eyes or shook heads.
"Can't see an entrance from here let's surf the canopy and get in closer, just watch for any flying fangs." Lukas pulled down his CAP control arm.
"WOW." Caron lifted off.
"Take it easy try and glide rather than walk on air, just like we done in training, that's it." Jack offered some calming guidance.
"OooOKaaayyy, got it." Caron swooped down almost hitting treetops.
"Slow down." Lukas gestured at Maggie and Wayne to pursue her, a task Jack had already volunteered for.
"Butterflies," Dharma grinned.
"You and your… Fan out guys, Dharma, Arten with me." Lukas dived from the ledge, skimming above tree tops as if he were born to fly.
"Nasties taking to the air," Maggie warned.

Stopping at a hover, Maggie drew her sidearm letting off two shots at flying snakes with crocodile heads. In response; a flash of green light pulsed from the pyramid hitting her right side. Maggie's arm wrenched back, power cells of her weapon exploding; spraying a molten red hot sidearm over her helmet and suit. She fell spinning, crashing through tree tops, branches splintering from her impact. Wayne fired at the second serpent stunning it before he catapulted backward under force of another pulse of green light hitting his shoulder. Snatching at several giant palm leaves Wayne halted his fall.

"DIVE, DOWN, DOWN." Lukas yelled as pulses flashed by Tyler and himself.
"What the hell!" Tyler plummeted amidst tree bark splintering, explosions of leaves under fire of whatever guarded the pyramid.
"Keep your heads down." Lukas scrambled to the shelter of boulders with Dharma and Arten. "Maggie, you okay? Wayne? Caron? Jack?" Chunks of rock showered around him.
"I'm okay. I can see an entrance from here." Caron crouched behind a tree.
"You just stay put." Lukas noted, but had no time to question why the finger tips of Arten's gloves had been ripped open.
"My, my arms messed up." Maggie lay holding her shoulder amongst leafy branches that had followed her down, "Weapons melted into my hand." She breathed heavily, while puffs of pain dulling drugs tickled her neck.
"Under fire Captain, need to find me a hole." Tyler sprinted from one tree to another, earth and fern debris showering around him as he ran.
"Damn tree's getting dissected." Wayne slid down a palm that erupted overhead.
"Fine here Lukas, I can see Caron." Jack peered through the rotting hole in a fallen tree. "Keep down girl, Spiderman's on his way."
"Jack stay put. Tyler, your just east of Maggie can you get over there?" Lukas tried to make sense of motion sensor displaying various colored dots moving around.
"You keep right outta my zone Tyler, ain't nothing shooting at me." Maggie picked melted weaponry from her glove.
"You okay?" Jack threw himself at Caron after dodging and weaving his way to her as fast as he could run.
"Yes, guess I'm not worthy of attention." Caron could hardly avoid gazing into Jack's eyes as he held her, pinned to the ground, helmets now all that prevented lips from diving at each other.

"Could be motion activated." Lukas pondered, his idea received with splinters of rock pinging off his helmet. "Guess not!"
"It didn't fire at Jack once, or me." Caron pointed out.
"Hey, HEY where the heck!" Lukas nearly had a fit at the sight of Arten wandering in the pyramid's direction. "Get down before you're blown down."
"I'm no threat Mr Lukas, you are the ones with weapons."
"Oh great, guess we'll have to use sharp sticks from now on! Disarm your weapons, guys, remove power cells." The Captain ejected power cells throwing his sidearm into bushes.
"Instant headache relief!" Wayne peered out from behind a tree.
"Tyler, Wayne go help Maggie. You two wait for me." Lukas chased after the twins.
"I think it's safe to get up now, don't you?" Caron blinked at the man on top of her.
"Your wish is my reluctant command." Jack stood, bowed and offered a hand pulling Caron to her feet.
"Do I get three wishes?"
"Do what I can."
"Hmmmm." Caron looked him up and down, grinning she proceeded to the pyramid's pillared entrance.

With Wayne and Tyler escorting Maggie back to Huntress, Alpha One gathered at the pyramid's entrance. Thirty feet high columns stood like two rows of sentinels guarding a path to doors at the far end of what felt like an empty hanger bay. They moved in, some watched for anything that might open fire, while other helmet lights scanned for revelations as to the nature of those who built it. The tunnel provided neither, just doors that now bared their way. Caron examined markings, but could make no sense of the language and no amount of pushing would move what resembled caste iron doors.

"Obviously out to lunch, yeah see there it says back in five million years." Lukas grew tired of standing around. "OPEN SESAME," he mimicked some muscle bound mythical Greek athlete as the command echoed from the tunnel into jungle, where it was also ignored, with the exception of one very distraught reptile whose nest had been blasted.

"I guess we can wait, I spy with my little eye something beginning with P." Jack gazed around not wanting to give anyone a clue.
"Pain in the…" Lukas parked just that on the floor with his back against a column.
"Must have something to do with this hole, can't see anything in there though." Caron crouched peering into a circular hole, about a foot deep. "My hand fits in there, can't feel anything." She returned to a vain attempt at interpreting shapes forming some kind of language.
"Looks simple enough to me." Jack stood back with hands on his hips "T, H, F, E, that looks like an M." he pointed at shapes formed from vertical, horizontal and diagonal lines, around which a variety of dots and dashes, varying in length, were set within squares, giving the appearance of tiles all the same size.
"Ya silly me," Caron swatted Jack's arm "Plonker, go and sit with your friend Berkules over there and let me think."
"I feel nothing from this," Dharma ran her hands over tiles.
"Perhaps it feels nothing from us," Arten retracted his helmet and gloves.
"That might not be wise kid." Lukas felt uneasy at Arten putting a bare hand into the hole. "And what happened to your gloves, I noticed they are damaged?"
"It, feels, tingly." Arten, ignoring the Captain, looked up at Jack and then whipped his hand out as doors creaked, slowly swinging inward.
"Well done kid," Jack patted Arten on the shoulder.
"Sounds like many doors opening Mr Lukas." Dharma tilted her head to one side, the crystalline nature of their bone structure made the twins very sensitive to all vibrations.
"We obviously have security clearance of some kind, I mean bugs must have crawled into that hole from time to time, it didn't open when your gloves were on so it's bio activated in some way… DNA coding security clearance just as we have." Jack reached into a belt pouch retrieving Sniffer. "Okay Sniffer, find Thoth and return."

The long passage ahead offered little but featureless stone walls. Only in a few places the alien languages offered further examination, not that it left Caron any the wiser. They waited at a junction for half an hour, eating supplies. A left passage led upwards, to the right downwards, it was certainly not Caron's idea of digging around in a pit, every shard of the past offering insights to secrets long buried. No, all they could do is wait for Sniffer to return. While remaining in sight of others Caron wandered up the left passage discovering more doors with a familiar hole. Despite both her, Arten and Dharma placing hands in holes these doors would not open. Upon return Sniffer caused a stir, glowing as he was, yet this soft glow brightly lit the passage. Sniffer could offer no data as to this new ability or where it had been obtained, Alpha One had to be satisfied with the news that he'd found Thoth's DNA trace and watched a monotonous holographic replay of its search.

"What was that?" Lukas's tired senses were jolted into life when the projection flashed white.
"Dunno but this must be where Sniffer found DNA trace." Jack scrutinized the image of a square room. "Sniffer, replay entrance to that projected room."
"Oww my eyes." Caron complained at the bright white flash just as Sniffer entered the room.
"Sorry guys, turn away for a minute, I have to see what caused that flash. Sniffer reverse sequence at tenth speed to one minute before this point." Jack squinted in anticipation of bright light.
"Unable to comply."
"You can't rewind?" Jack looked up at the droid.
"No data for specified time."
"What you forgot or something!"
"No data."
"I think our little droid here has been messed with, maybe whatever that flash was knocked him out for a while." Lukas speculated. "Sniffer, analyze time sequence upon entering room and display."
"Yep there's almost nine minutes missing." Jack gave Lukas an expression of 'we are not alone'.
"There's obviously advanced technology hidden away behind those doors and we know this place is very capable of defending its secrets, so we ain't gonna push the matter. They, whoever they are, don't want us to know what happened to Sniffer here and pursuing

that mystery could be dangerous." At this point Lukas was acutely aware of having only civilians in his party.

"Yeah, going down there makes the hairs on my neck stand high," Jack gazed down the sloping passageway.

"We have to find answers somehow." Although nervous about the prospect they all knew Caron was right. "Perhaps the twins could sense danger?"

"There is little sense here Miss Caron." Dharma looked as blank as the feelings she gained.

"Sniffer, display sample location again… Enlarge." Jack moved around the projection looking for anything that might suggest their next move.

"Same ol language with no context" Caron sighed "Got my work cut out here."

"Sniffer, zoom into sample… there's nothing there." All Jack could see was the texture of a stone floor.

"Wait a minute could have sworn I saw something, Sniffer, zoom out, display trace site floor… OHH, now that's more like it." At last Caron had a picture to look at. "No language with it though."

"Those circles, would you say that's the Sirius system Captain?" Jack swept an arm over a projection of large and small circles covering the floor.

"That's could well be Sirius A at room centre, yeah right number of planets, can't recall how many moons there should be. That would put us here I think." He pointed to one circle "No, can't be, looks like there's two moons." Lukas rubbed his chin, "So where the hell are we then, no doesn't add up."

"Could this world have had two moons?" Arten suggested.

"Guess it's feasible." Lukas looked doubtful.

"Sniffer, date the etching of these circles." Jack yawned as stimulants began to wear off.

"Approximately two hundred years."

"And the wall markings."

"Approximately one hundred to one hundred and twenty thousand years."

"This has been here that long!?" Caron's eyes widened.

"And those circles were added relatively recently. That's a blatant trail for us to follow wouldn't you say?" Jack turned to the others." Sniffer indicate where sample was found with a red dot please."

"Slap bang in the middle of that moon, is that the existing one or the vanished one though?" Lukas rubbed his shaven head.
"Whatever the case that moon was here at least two hundred years ago, perhaps we should question the natives." Jack pondered, "Sniffer, what did you obtain the sample from?"
"No data."
"Sniffer, sample was extracted from the bare stone floor was it?" Jack tried to ascertain what the sample was, hair, skin cell or some form of container that preserved it.
"Negative."
"Sniffer, then what was it gained from you ping pong?"
"No data."
"Oh great, whatever it was doesn't want us to know about it." Jack sighed "Have we got anymore of that pick me up spray stuff, my brain is saying night, night."
"There's more doors leading off that room." Dharma pointed out.
"Okay, okay. Sniffer, return to room where DNA trace was found, walking speed, show us the way." Lukas sprayed everyone's necks, rapidly reviving the party.

Their trek through a labyrinth was far shorter than expected, much of what Sniffer had explored led to dead ends and therefore Alpha One was spared many hours of retracing their steps again and again. Inaccessible rooms or passageways gave rise to many questions as to what this complexes purpose was. Finally they arrived at least a hundred feet below ground level, approaching the room with caution, it offered no surprises.

"Well there's no trace of DNA on the floor now. Sniffer isn't capable of extracting the DNA, only finding and scanning it. So what have you been up to glowbot eh?" Jack glared at the droid.
"Nope, doors won't open." Caron leant against a wall frustrated.
"Could that second moon be a ship?" Lukas crouched by the circle presumed to be the planet they were exploring.
"Sniffer, find Thoth." Jack threw his hands out to the side, slapping them down against thighs in a gesture of frustration.
"Searching." Sniffer shot passed Caron and into a door hole.
"Okay, what's the game here!?" Lukas took a step back as doors opened and Sniffer proceeded into the next room.

"Sniffer, Return." Jack yelled.
"Stay put everyone." Lukas gestured for them to come away from the door.
"Sniffer display sample fifteen of Thoth's DNA." Jack gazed at the hologram he'd seen many times. "Sniffer, display a sample of your DNA." He turned to catch the expression on everyone's faces, though no one had twigged yet "HA! Caught you out you little sucker!"
"A bot with… DNA?" Lukas caught on to Jack's trick command.
"Exactly, couldn't have opened that door without absorbing the DNA trace and… if I'm not mistaken this is a full double helix unlike all the other samples we have." Jack eyed the droid suspiciously.
"So.. Thoth laid a Sniffer egg or what? How on Earth, or anywhere else for that matter, could a bunch of clank absorb living matter like that?" Lukas glared at the glowing sphere. "Dharma, can you feel anything from this?"
"It's, it's very strong." Dharma stepped toward Sniffer reaching a hand out to touch it. "I feel faint, I…"
"Okay enough." Caron held Dharma as a mother might comfort a frightened daughter. "The balls obviously not for messing with."
"Perhaps we should proceed before whatever changes its mind." Jack suggested.

Whereas Alpha One's access had revealed little more than stone walls, this room offered a taste of hidden technology. At its centre a cross of four black consoles displayed luminous markings of an alien language. The Northern displayed an M, Southern W, Western E and Eastern an E reversed. Each had varying numbers of dots and dashes, some luminescent while others very gradually began to glow or increase as would a meter reading pressure or energy levels. At cross centre a silver metallic circle with two closed lids resembled an eye. Above this a hole in the ceiling. While Jack and Lukas pondered over technology, Caron was immediately drawn to the far wall.

"Egyptian, at least in style." She examined a wall painting depicting a pyramid with a line rising from its cap stone up to a bird surrounded by stars. "The Heron, Bennu, spirit of Ra, what most know as the Phoenix." Caron explained.

"So what do you think it means?" Jack placed a hand on her shoulder.

"In the context of this place I don't know, but the whole deal with Bennu is guidance, creation and destruction, life and death…"

"Sounds ominous," Lukas became more concerned about the luminous readings around a contraption that now seemed to have connections with life and death.

"Later stories of the Phoenix put things into perspective a bit more. However the Bennu had close ties to the pyramids, in that the cap stone IS the Bennu or Ben Ben stone, its radiant light, the spirit of Ra illuminates all. In creation myths the Bennu is the bird perched on the first land, a primordial mound which is the cap stone…"

"And Mike believes these pyramids have something to do with terraforming." Lukas felt a sense of dread, wondering if they'd set some device in motion that would have traumatic consequences.

"Pyramids symbolize evolution, the steps of life, each life we are refined through experience until we reach the pinnacle, and there we find Bennu, spirit of God. Bennu holds the secret of immortality." Caron turned to see if anyone else felt a sense of being way, way out of their depth, lurking in the basement of gods.

"Oh.. So perhaps that's why we are only given access to certain parts of the pyramid, while Thoth's DNA gave us access to more." Jack's tension lightened, as the detective in him fitted mental pieces of this puzzle together.

"Makes sense, but what of this?" Lukas gestured to the four terminals. "How does Bennu relate to that device, other than laying a glowing egg?" He gestured at Sniffer.

"Hmm, well, in the later legend of Phoenix it gathers elements, fragrances, herbs and spices, which refer to alchemy, builds a nest from these elements, they erupt into flames under the gaze of Ra, the Sun god, purifying the elements, consuming Phoenix's physical form. What remains is an egg, which represents either personal consciousness, the sum total of our awareness and experience, or that of a race, so the egg is then the Earth; the human races sphere of experience. From it rises a serpent which relates to Earthly wisdom, that transforms into a new Phoenix. It takes the egg shell, nest, whatever it has transformed into pure knowledge, to the sun temple in Heliopolis, there to dwell for a time."

"Right, okay and in the real world that means what?" Lukas tried to fit all this into his uncomplicated approach to things.

"The whole thing is about evolution, and eventual ascension to a higher state of being, of existence, pyramid, Bennu, Phoenix. Right from the first mound," Caron raised her arms gesturing at the pyramid they were under. "To ascending from the world into the stars, from dense physical energy into light. As Einstein put it; energy never dies, it transforms from one state to another."

"Perhaps this device is a transport system of some kind?" Jack peered up into the hole above terminals. "Goes way up there, probably to the cap stone, too far to see anyway."

"So we flick the on switch and go sit on the cap stone, is that what you're suggesting?"

"I doubt if it's quite that simple boss but something in that general ball park, just a thought." Jack shrugged.

"These could indicate directions." Caron walked around terminals. "North, South East and West, dots might indicate degrees, lines height, depth or whatever you pilots call it."

"Could be, could be." Jack nodded.

"Hmm, okay let's take what we have, feed it to the computers and science specialists see what they can make of it and that mutant droid." Lukas took one last gaze around the room.

--*--

Breakfast aboard Argo brought with it pressure from sections of the crew. With little to do other than guard scientists on the planet, which didn't occupy enough restless marines, and those who weren't engrossed with data to analyze hounded Captain Griffin, who finally relented to pressure; giving orders for shore leave, or any leave provided they leave him alone. Locating a reasonably safe island, Huntress offloaded it's cargo of thrilled tourists.

Caron sat in soft sand, arms holding knees to her chest as she watched crew in their more natural habitat, other than those on guard duty there were no suits. It felt good to feel sunlight and the breeze on her gently tanned skin, feel sand under her feet. Voices near and far rather than the set volume suits provided, no matter how far away someone was. Indeed some of the sounds here made her laugh inside; Maggie and McThug trading insults, Sonya screaming as Zack chased her, distant shouts from those playing hoverball. What Yun and Arten were saying was beyond range, their closeness and smiles said a lot, while they watched something in a rock pool. Dharma seemed happy, alone with everything she touched, from a grain of sand to the ocean she gazed out at now. Oh there were those gazing at her beauty, just as fire can enchant, but few are foolish enough to touch.

"Sure you don't want any?" Jack sat next to her with a plate of barbequed shell fish. "Good stuff."
"No, maybe later.. Oh go on then just one bite."
"Open wide."
"Mmm, bit chewy but tastes better than shrimp, guess they'll be simulating that to."
"Be sick of it by the time we get home." Jack set the plate down, knowing he would be tempted by another taste soon enough.
"Love is in the air." She spied on Lukas and Kartha pretending to discus recent events, and not what was really on their minds.
"Yeah, guess you could say natures in full force here. Man meet wo-man." Jack nudged his head towards Maggie and McThug "Me got big club, you come see."
"Oh I thought you'd never ask," Caron smirked.
"I was waiting for a dragon to snatch you away so I could rescue you."
"On your white steed with the big lance and shiny armor?"
"Well dammit that was meant to be a surprise."
"So does Sir Jack have any kids?"
"Yeah, er, no." he looked away, gazing out to sea.
"Oh sorry, touchy subject?" Caron sank her toes into sand, feeling tense.
"They, my wife and kids; Lance and Amy were amongst many victims of the tsunami in Australia. She, Maria was visiting her Sister over there when it hit."
"Oh I'm sorry Jack." Caron placed her hand on his; resting in the sand.
"Oh I'm sure I'm far from being the only one to loose people here, heck we are the lucky few." He gazed out at waves "I try not to think about it, it was six years ago, well two hundred and

whatever, but the ghosts still haunt ya know."
"Must be…"
"What about you?"
"Ha, no." Caron bit her lip, "never had time for all that, you know, married to my dusty ol books, or digging up something. I don't know about the rest of my family."
"Must have been a Spiderman in your life at some point?" A smile returned to his face.
"Yeah right, would need to be larger than life to keep up with me. No, relationships have not been on my agenda, even at university I studied obsessively, no time for boy distractions."
"What you mean you've never… not even a brief; love you but I must go deal?"
"Well that's always the fear isn't it? Fall in love and out of freedom. I always sailed with life Jack, just didn't allow any ship to dock in my port, as it were."
"Oh." Jack was lost for words especially at the sight of those gorgeous legs flowing out of tight shorts and shapely, well shapely everything with a hint of divine modesty sculpting her form. "Man hath been denied Heaven," his thoughts escaped.
"Why thank you kind Sir." She kissed his cheek.
"I shalt not wash for a year and a day."
"That's a terrible attempt at an English accent, and I would suggest washing if you want another one." Caron gazed skyward raising her eyebrows.
"You must have had a crush on someone at least, tell me that much or I'll test your DNA for alien influences!"
"Pfft, might surprise us both. No I mean there's been some butt watching, you know, I wouldn't exactly say I've been totally switched off… far from it."
"Waiting for Mr Right then?"
"Mr out of sight might be a more apt description. Some part of me belongs somewhere else, I have strange dreams at times, have done all my life."
"Dreams are often strange, abstract, like a personal symbolic language, well you would know that." Jack's gaze turned to admiring Caron again, still finding it difficult to believe no one had touched such beauty.
"Yes, but it's the feeling… almost like I'm haunting myself, or that

there's a me somewhere else calling, trying to show me the way, yet I can never find it." Caron's gaze fell under the weight of uncertainties.

"Hi guys," Lukas knelt in front of them "I'm afraid duty calls, it seems the clock is ticking."

"Ticking?" Jack's eyebrows raised.

"Yes, we haven't been able to make much progress, but analysis of the terminals you discovered indicates that something is imminent." Kartha knelt by Lukas.

"That thing is charging, dashes are almost fully illuminated and all but a few dots are glowing." Lukas added.

"Comparing their levels to when you found the device, we estimate that something's going to happen in less than five hours." Kartha looked worried.

"So it's all hands on deck I'm afraid, can't leave anyone down here despite Natasha threatening mutiny." Lukas grinned. "I'm sure we can all catch some more sun tomorrow though, or as soon as we analyze whatever this thing does."

"Ohh, well that was nice while it lasted." Caron stood up brushing sand from her butt.

"Huntress will be here in about twenty five minutes so pick up your trash guys. Lukas and Kartha wandered off to round up more crew.

"I, err, kidding aside, you know" Jack wished he'd had a little rum for Dutch courage "Well I know your life has been devoted to work, but things are different now wouldn't you say?"

"I haven't really thought about life, the future or anything, it's all been about the now Jack, but yeah, the big picture isn't one of digging up the past, more like surviving another day, or another generation I guess."

"I'd like to share that with you," Jack turned Caron to face him.

"I, I," Caron's eyes broke contact with his "I do really like being with you Jack."

"But."

"But, it's difficult to explain, there's something I need to complete, within me, an answer I have to find before I could possibly answer a question such as yours Jack."

"I understand, just friends eh?" He released her arm.

"No, you don't understand, I barely understand what I feel. I'm

quite used to saying no Jack, I'm not brushing you off, I just can't say yes."
"Well you know I have other people to interview for the position." Jack grinned through a heavy heart.
"Ohh do you now, come on lets just paddle in the water while we can." She took his hand and smiled although something kicked, screamed and cried within her.

--*--

Argo waited and watched as tension grew amongst crew members. Captain Griffin strummed fingers on the arm of his command chair, his gaze pulled toward Kartha who had already snatched it on several occasions, provoking an inner smile. Everyone on the Bridge waited for instruments to show some activity. Yoto simply wandered from console to console looking over shoulders.

"How much longer Mike, are you sure about those estimates?" Lukas offered an entirely different gaze to Mike sitting at his side.
"Not exactly a precise art estimating alien technology Captain, but it shouldn't be too long now."
"Good, I don't want to be late for my retirement party." Lukas sighed.

"Well this is fun!" Caron felt uncomfortable in the science lab's silence, watching a huge screen displaying stars above the planets crescent.
"What's up kid, why the long face?" Jack asked of the solemn Arten.
"Me thinks a Sister doth tease too much." Caron twitched her head toward Dharma.
"Ahh, well, humor in the face of tickling kid, laugh it off. Perhaps sharing secrets might disarm the threat of their deployment?" Jack advised.
"Even us Earth troggs are not completely blind Arten, you have feelings for someone don't you?" Caron was answered with a smile that Arten could not hold back. "Does Yun know about your feelings?"
"No he won't tell her." Dharma crossed her eyes and sighed.

"Well…" Caron was silenced by an alarm.

"Okay," Lukas sat up in his chair as a shaft of golden light shot up from the planet's surface reaching a point five hundred miles directly in front of Argo "about time." He watched light radiating from the shafts tip forming a circular aura. "Getting anything?"
"Slight increase in gravitation Sir." Heather glared nervously at her console.
"It's a circle!" Lukas stood up "You getting this Jack?"
"Yes, no moon that's our circle, looks like its growing."
"Well at least that's one mystery… solll" Lukas fell back into his seat.
"Gravity, massive gravitational forces Captain." Yoto held onto the back of Heather's seat.
"Shit GET US OUTTA HERE." Lukas felt the ship vibrating.
"Vortex forming dead ahead." Heather's console displayed swirling energy patterns and warning indicators.
"We're being pulled in Sir." Kartha glanced up at the main screen.
"Full reverse thrusters." Lukas grasped chair arms, helmets activated as Argo shuddered.
"It could be a worm hole forming Captain."
"That's just great Mike, see you in the next life then! Bring her about and throttle us out of this."
"She won't respond Sir, we're being pulled in." Kartha increased port thrusters to maximum, despite Argo fighting to escape the vortex's grasp, massive forces steadily drew her in.
"Can't fight it Captain, can't maneuver, I'm sure that device has a destination in mind so fighting it might not be a good idea." Mike reasoned with Lukas, as Argo's speed dramatically increased, thrusters blazing in defiance as they passed through the circle of light, an eye in space.
"Very well, kill the thrusters. Any idea where we're going, because our trajectory looks a bit too close to Sirius A for my liking?"
"Destination determined." Kartha checked and rechecked data not wanting to accept it "ETA three minutes fifteen seconds… Sir."
"Well don't keep us in suspense Kartha, where's our next vacation?"
"There Captain," Yoto zoomed in on Sirius B "Impact in two minutes fifty nine seconds."

"Can we fire weapons at that pyramid, stop this damn hell ride to oblivion?" Lukas stood up.
"If we launched missiles they would impact about an hour after we are long gone. They'd be under the same gravity vice and we would need a thousand Argo's to scratch the surface of that Sir." Kartha replied, despite knowing the might of Argo's weaponry, she knew Argo was no match for a star many times harder than diamond.
"Then I guess Bennu has our destination set for death." Lukas gazed defiantly at the rapidly growing white orb.

"If I say yes will you make it stop?" Caron held Jack, a tear almost escaped her eyes before being taken care of. "Dammit she hit controls on her arm, finally managing to retract the helmet; Jack and the twins doing likewise.
"It's okay Miss Caron." Dharma touched her arm briefly, then turning to Arten as Caron's trembling lips met Jack's.
"Twelve seconds." The console shared unwanted information.
"Ten, nine."
"Sorry about the teasing Arten." Dharma held his hand "I think its beautiful, you and Yun."
"Five, four,"
"Goodbye Jack, I, I." Caron closed her eyes, as Argo became indistinct in the stars radiance.
"Two, one."

Chapter Eight: Man's Folly

Visions cascaded through Caron's mind, time, space, ten thousand lives all fell like snowflakes upon the landscape of her consciousness. A whisper called, beckoned for her soul to walk corridors of time. Caron wandered between two worlds, one inner, one outer, unsure of which was real. Following a light surrounded by light, somehow knowing where to go and what to do. It all seemed like a dream, Caron questioned if she was sleepwalking, but didn't fight it, she couldn't, she had to follow the light through this chamber, floating now, floating away.

"Miiiister Jaaack." He heard the angelic vision calling to him, thinking it looked so much like that girl Dharma. Of course it must be her in death. Jack wondered why he still felt like crap even though he was dead, perhaps faint echoes of his body dieing, yes that made sense. "Mister Jack wake up," and there was Arten.

"Where is Caron?" Jack asked in a slurred, drowsy manner. "It's so bright here," he lifted a numb arm to shield his eyes unsure if he were laying up, down, standing, floating, no he could feel pressure on his back, must be laying down, and there was Dharma above him "Hi." Jack returned Dharma's smile, her clear diamond teeth sparkling, a rare sight bringing some clarity to the misty white blur of limited vision. "Odd." Jack thought aloud, trying to focus eyes, although now only seeing curved lips of Dharma's broad smile.

"Uuugghhh." Lukas groaned, trying to bring his senses back, feeling the arm of his command seat. "Are we nearly there yet?" He joked, opening one eye to what seemed a heavenly scene.
"I… I guess so." Mike patted himself to see if he still had physical form.
"Guess I must have done something right, thought I'd be greeted with pitch forks and fire." Lukas retracted his helmet "I at least expected a brief second of agonizing pain."
"Don't know about agony, but I feel like I've just been yanked out of my body and thrown back in upside down." Heather sat with head in hands.

"It's unreal." Kartha slowly stood with other Bridge crew, staring before the main screen at gigantic crystalline formations glowing with a white radiance.

"Right, so where are we, dare I ask?" Lukas tried to grasp reality and hold on for all he was worth. "Are we alive even?" He checked readings on his suits arm.

"Guess so." Mike pinched his cheeks, still not convinced.

"Picking up life signs out there, just one." Heather tried to focus uncooperative eyes on her console panel. "No, sorry must be a glitch, or me."

"Well navigational instruments not making a whole lot of sense Heather." Kartha's attention darted from one data display to the next. "Best I can tell you is that we are here Captain," she pointed to the screen.

"You're a genius! Any other useless information… anyone?" Lukas still felt dizzy, despite numerous shots of hypo spray trying to correct bodily functions.

"We are in some form of cavern, no way in, no way out, sensor sweeps just bounce back. Nearest matter analysis is diamond, although it's way off the density scale, whatever that mineral is, it makes diamond look like putty. Temperature 50 degrees, zero gravity." Heather shrugged.

"If it didn't sound insane I would say we are within Sirius B." Mike hesitantly offered.

"Insane counts right now Mike. Damage report?"

"No reports of injuries, all systems functional." Yoto continued checking systems analysis.

"Have all science personnel meet me in the conference room." Lukas took a last glance at gigantic crystals on the screen before leaving. "With me Mike."

"Okay take a seat people." Mike activated floor sections, which elevated to provide benches for science personnel filing into the conference room.

"We have ourselves a real mind bender here." Lukas gestured to the screen capturing both eyes and minds of those present. "We are stuck in this cavern, or whatever it is. As you can see," He displayed what data sensors could provide, "While being fascinating it doesn't make any sense. Arten, Dharma, perhaps you

could shed some light on this for..?"
"Caron?" Jack entered looking around to no avail.
"Is there a problem Jack?" Lukas scanned faces searching for Caron.
"Ah yeah, can't find Caron. She was with us in our lab before whatever happened, but I can't find her now."
"I think she has gone Mr. Jack." Arten opened his eyes.
"Gone, what do you mean?" Jack stood at the door.
"Gone." Arten pointed to the screen.
"What the... Caron Foster report immediately." Lukas paused for an answer "Attention all personnel locate Miss Caron Foster."
"What's the issue Sir?" Anwar marched along deck four looking in every room as he went.
"No idea Lieutenant, she's missing, that's all we know. Activate delta droids, deny access to all airlocks."
"Captain, it's possible she was the life sign Heather detected, I rechecked the data. An airlock was used while we were unconscious. Life sign vanished at, uh, zero nine point one five." Yoto reported.
"JACK, hold it, JACK" Lukas yelled at the figure running toward a gravity well. Arten stop him, Dharma, stop her."
"Ahhgh." Jack faltered, stumbling to the floor, holding his head.
"I can't find.. She is beyond me Mr Lukas." Dharma stood in the corridor with eyes closed, perceiving confusing thoughts and a mind that would not respond.
"Damn fool, get up, what did you think you were gonna do?" Lukas grabbed Jack by the scruff of his collar.
"Well if you think I'm gonna sit here and play patta-cake, you can stick your command where the sun don't shine." Jack's glare passed from Lukas to Arten.
"Alright, alright calm down. Going out there would pose an unreasonable risk Jack, we'll deploy droids that can search faster than we could. C'mon, you can monitor the search from the Bridge." Lukas wanted Jack where he could keep an eye on him.
"Dharma, Arten join us and keep trying to contact her."

"Tunnel located at Caron's last known position." Jack reported.
"Sending six delta droids in."
"I'm sure they will soon find her, she can't of gone far." Lukas

tried to reassure.

"Lost contact with droids." Jack turned back to face Lukas.
"Everything is reflected back from those crystals. The droids will return if they find anything." Heather informed Jack. "Picking up some strange readings Sir."
"Sir." Yoto pointed to the screen, which displayed bright points of colored light flying around the cavern.
"Okay, looks like we have company of some kind." Lukas felt uneasy watching blue, red and green lights darting around. "Any form of contact Yooookaaay, stay calm, stay calm." He felt anything but calm faced with what appeared on the Bridge, its massive ethereal wings extending out through walls. "Move slowly behind me guys, no sudden moves." Lukas felt the glare of red eyes upon him.
"Ahh, shiiiit." Kartha nearly leapt out of her skin as the beasts gargoyle like head turned to face her in a lightening sharp reaction to her movement, visible electronic pulses streaming from its horned head, down a thick neck into a remotely human and heavily muscular, semi translucent torso.
"We, we come in peace." Lukas felt stupid uttering such words, but they were all that came to a mind overwhelmed with dread.
"Ggggrrrrmmm." The beast's head turned sharply to a silver staff it brandished with a huge clawed fist, every move it made marked by electric impulses, as with any living creature, accept these were very visible. "HUMAN." Its thoughts thundered through the ship.
"Yes… We are humans, who…?" Lukas dared to admit.
"Gnnn, WHY HERE?" It snorted disdainfully, muscle bound reptilian legs advancing the biped closer to Lukas, it's beak now threateningly close to the Captain's face.
"We seek a being called Thoth." Arten felt he was somehow in the presence of a kindred spirit, vicious as the beast appeared to be, Arten could sense more.
"YOU, what are you?" The gargoyle's red eyes glared at Arten, wings folding against its back.
"Human descendant, third generation colonist from Sarfayon system." Mike informed.
"Interesting. Thoth not known…" The gargoyle paused as Arten projected images and what he knew of Thoth to the beast's mind.
"Gnnn, you wait." It vanished.

"WAIT! Shit, it might know where Caron is."
"Sorry Jack, kinda hard to think straight with that in your face." Lukas mentally kicked himself.
"It said wait, inferring that it would return." Kartha put an arm around Jack shoulders.

--*--

Caron woke to the blurred image of a woman's face staring at her. Before she could say anything the being opened white feathered wings and flew away. Caron felt smooth, cold crystal against her skin, sitting up she gazed down at silken white garments that almost blended and flowed from her into white crystal with a Selenite appearance; its structure glowing like fiber optics, reflecting light in a multitude of crystalline streams. Adjusting garments, feeling her breasts were a little too exposed, Caron surveyed her surroundings. Everything was white, a large room with columns reaching skyward, all made from the same crystalline substance. Sounds of bird song and a fountain echoed from walls beyond columns, it all seemed like a dream surreal heavenly. Knowing that Selenite, amongst other crystals and gems, were thought to have spiritual qualities of communication by mystics, simply added to Caron's presumption of a divine presence. A white dove, symbolic of the soul, perched upon a lectern facing rows of crystalline benches, between which she sat on an altar. Slipping her legs off the smooth bed of crystal, Caron quickly drew silk over her knees at the vague sight of a figure standing in a large doorway. Perhaps a dead relative come to greet her, she recalled various stories about death and the afterlife. No, no it was him, was she dead or just dreaming again? No, they had died, that was right, crashing into that star.

"Am I dead or just dreaming?" Caron spoke softly to the approaching figure, still unable to focus on his features, though she could make out a human masculine form wearing white robes like those of ancient Greece, Rome or Egypt.
"Perhaps, but then life is said to be a dream in the mind of our creator, is it not?"
"Yes, well I'd like to wake up... Oh, then I, of course." Death was

the other option she concluded, squinting at the man. "The afterlife." Caron gazed around accepting what she had feared.
"After life? What a strange term. Define life?" He crossed arms over his chest.
"Breathing… well, consciousness." Caron shrugged.
"Are you conscious?"
"I guess… But…"
"Your time is not up yet Caron, you are very much in a land of the living."
"Then if I'm not dead or dreaming you…" Caron's heart pounded. "You are the one haunting me, my Prince, you are real?"
"I have been that amongst others you have known from time to time, or as you would call it 'life to life' Priestess." He stood before her, gazing into Caron's eyes.
"THOTH!" Caron bowed without thinking.
"Oh come, come, I thought humans had seen the folly of worship." Thoth lifted her chin..
"History runs deep." Past lives flashed through her mind, accepting Thoth's hand she stood by his side.
"Indeed." He led her from the pronaos.
"Where am I?" Caron's bare feet padded on crystal floors.
"Canatra. Greeks called it Olympus." Thoth's free hand swept across the scene before them.
"Domain of the gods!" Caron's jaw dropped at the sight of huge pyramids, what she thought to be temples, grandiose architectural landmarks graced by ornate gardens.
"So men say." He led her down wide steps into gardens "This is a domain that embraces many aspects of Earth and similar worlds, or at least the more inspiring and virtuous aspects of them. Please sit." Thoth gestured to a stone bench that circled a fountain, from which a little waterfall cascaded over stones, flowing away along a stream winding through miniature trees and shrubs.
"I saw an angel, she flew away." Caron recalled her waking moments.
"An angel indeed!" Thoth's smile was prompted by thoughts of 'if only you knew'. "You will meet many forms here, do not be alarmed."
"What like aliens from other worlds?"
"You are the only alien here. However, forms that have evolved on

other worlds are mirrored here, just as I am human, others may be." He gestured to a centaur statue.
"It's all so beautiful, peaceful." Caron began to relax a little. Mind and senses clear, she sought to ease their long torment and denial.
"I will return shortly." Thoth seemed distracted.
"Could I…?" Caron didn't know where to start "just a few minutes, I feel like I've waited an eternity for answers."
"Yes of course." Thoth sat next to her, his bronzed hand holding Caron's.
"What are you to me? I mean you're a…" She stopped herself from saying god "an immortal being probably more evolved than I can imagine, and I'm a half witted human, yet you haunt my dreams, I feel like we have been together many times?"
"Your dreams are perhaps mingled with memories. I am immortal, but then so are you. My kind reform continuously whereas beings of your domain rebirth, your form has a different way of regenerating. Within us all is a soul that is our divine, eternal self, in a sense it learns to create a more and more evolved physical form through which it experiences and learns from existence. One day beings like yourself, will become like my race. And we in turn will evolve to a higher form." Thoth nodded toward an obelisk.
"OHH my, is it?" Her eyes widened in wonder at a pure white bird, it's tail feathers akin to those of a peacock, although semi translucent; shimmering as would a mirage or fire fanned by a breeze.
"Bennu, yes, or Phoenix if you prefer, Ho O, or a multitude of other names, some of which are not pronounceable with these vocal chords. They are not governed by the same physics as third dimensional beings." Thoth pointed to a roof top, smiling at another Phoenix "They like to watch."
"I thought there was only one?"
"There is, each being is like a flame of a greater fire, a unified consciousness. Each has its own experiences, thoughts, character, yet they all feel as one. You are a human of humanity, yet to be one with all your kind."
"I never thought it was a real creature, just something symbolic, it's so beautiful, enchanting."
"It is, in many ways, I would ask that if it should approach you, please avert your eyes, do not gaze into his, hers." Thoth shrugged

"Their polarity, what you call gender, can change in the blink of an eye."
"Okay, it's safe to look at him from a distance though?"
"Yes, that one, has not visited your world, so he may be curious."
"Phoenix's have visited Earth?" Caron turned, admiring Thoth's face.
"They can become a human consciousness yes. Born within you, seeing through your eyes, feeling your thoughts. My kind aren't the only ones to walk among you."
"And you, how did you walk with me?"
"Ah affairs of the heart stir you. We have been lovers, relations, acquaintances, through some of your lives Caron, you are a very loving spirit and perhaps I am guilty in some way of caging that."
"I've felt that I cannot truly love another, that we are bound in some way." Tears threatened to flow.
"We have been very close and I have no doubt we will again, in another time, another place, but your spirit must grow, you must live and know that love is not a possession, it is a gift to share. It is only then that we become one with anything, including ourselves."
"I don't know what to feel then, I am lost again." Caron's wore a pleading expression.
"I will clear your mind of these torments Caron." Thoth stroked her hair "And you must live, and be free, be life."
"But I love you, I know I have carried you in here." She held his hand to her heart "life after life."
"I know, and you have loved others, you love another now."
"You know then. I don't know who I'm betraying, it tears me to pieces."
"One is felt by the soul, another by your heart. The soul will find me eventually, your heart has one life, and you must live it. There are many ways to love Caron, there is no betrayal in loving us both, in different ways."
"Surely you are aware that life for my kind is not a hopeful prospect?" Caron began to feel more at ease as Thoth stroked her hair and her mind.
"Indeed. Do you feel better?"
"Yes, strange, I feel there are things to do that I've put off for too long. Odd."
"Good, good, what has passed between us has passed, what maybe,

maybe, walk forward along your path and cherish what you find." Thoth smiled.

"What happened, where are my colleagues, Jack and…"

"Oh the feather landed safely, you need not worry. Now enjoy the sunshine, Larasi will keep you company, while I speak with your friends." Thoth raised a finger as if to say 'NO'.

"Ohh." Caron gulped "Hell, hello." She felt overwhelmed by the winged woman that presented herself with a smile.

"Do you like them?" Larasi fanned out white feathered wings.

"Took me three… weeks to grow, it is weeks isn't it? My English is a bit corroded metal."

"Rusty? Well there's four weeks to our lunar cycle, orbit thingy so…"

"That's it. Stand up for me let's have a look at you."

"You grew them?"

"Yes, we adapt to different forms, depends where we are going to visit. Been a long time since I visited your world. Turn around for me."

"Would I recognize you, in our history?" Caron slowly twirled wondering why she was being examined.

"I forget now, I became the goddess of gatherings, naughty ones, you know, what's the word."

"Orgies!?"

"Yes that's it, what was my name, hmm, oh well let's get you ready for visitors shall we, needs some flow." Larasi floated up.

"Some grace and a little sparkle."

"I, err, okay."

--*--

"Still nothing from droids." Jack turned to a console "Dharma anything?" His gaze fell across a shoulder at Dharma who seemed surprised, pointing above Jack.

"Wha.." Jack looked up as an ostrich feather landed on his face.

"Geezz… its, its real!" His fingers stroked soft luminescent barbs.

"Odd to say the least!" Lukas moved to Jack's side frowning.

"Its from…"

"THOTH!" Mike finished Jack's sentence, glaring at the screen.

"Holy shit!" Lukas remarked of a face that almost filled the cavern, staring back at them.

"Do we kneel or what?" Heather questioned.

"Oh I would, best start praying or you might invoke his wrath!" An unfamiliar voice turned heads of Bridge personnel towards the doors behind them. "Please don't leave your litter around." Thoth held up Sniffer, from which he'd regained his DNA.

"YOU!" Jack held up the feather. "It WAS you all those years ago." He recognized the form, shimmering just as it had done as he felt life slipping away on Logan Five.

"Hello, umm, your highness, we come in peace." Lukas blurted two out of four greetings to form in his head, that he now wanted to kick swiftly down the black hole he wished would appear.

"Peace, really! That is a pleasant surprise coming from those like yourselves." Thoth caught sight of the twins. "Oh, but what do we have here?" He approached a nervous Dharma, gazing as if seeing straight through her; not a million miles from the truth. "Now you, you offer a glimmer of hope." Thoth, standing almost seven feet tall, gently raised Dharma's chin with one finger. "Both of you, a remarkable transformation for humans and long, long overdue."

"May I..." Jack had only one question in his mind.

"Yes she is in good hands Jack. I shall return her to you, or you to her depending on what transpires." Thoth took Arten's hand, placing its palm against a wall "Close your eyes and think of mud, or sand... that's it, now press your hand into the mud... yes, good. Your nature is akin to that which surrounds you." He gestured to crystals on the main screen.

"That's solid trurium!" Mike could hardly believe a hand imprint sunk into the wall as if it were wet concrete.

"It is remarkable; we have not seen such a rapid genetic transformation of this nature before." Thoth's spirit lifted at the unknown, new phenomena to explore. "Seeders must be experimenting." He pondered. "You show signs of early, primitive evolutional traits, yet within quite an advanced being, hmm, yes." Thoth continued to gaze over and into the twins. "You have done well to follow me here."

"Then you are Thoth?" Jack felt a chill running down his spine, although nothing compared to what Arten had just felt through his entire crystalline skeletal structure.

"Yes."

"Sir I cannot express how relieved we are to finally meet you." Lukas stepped forward.
"Please sit" Thoth waved him down "I am a teacher not a god, sit, sit."
"If intellect is any measure of divinity then you are a god to us Thoth." Mike had given no thought as to what he would say in the unlikely event they ever met this mythical ancient being.
"Intellect is an insect crawling upon a mountain that is wisdom, science has a place, its how such is applied that counts. Humanity's wisdom is a fly on the dung hill of scientific catastrophe, and you would have me teach you anything?" Thoth glared at them.
"We only ask your help with one thing that threatens to end us all Sir. Since you were last among us much has changed, the Earth itself has taken vengeance on our stupidity. As if billions of lives were not enough, we have a genetic mutation that prevents conception." Lukas explained.
"What little facts we have lead us to believe that you know a great deal about genetics, that whatever being, you are immortal, at least to our concept of time. Your knowledge is humanities last hope." Mike pleaded their case.
"So the sands of time have run out for you, I feared as much. So near," Thoth turned to the twins "and yet so far." he glanced at the others. Your journey here was a test, though I wonder if you have Kahkuri blood on your hands and their gold in your pockets?"
"No certainly not, perhaps a few samples of their jewelry, but only in good measure with botanical, biological and mineral samples." Heather defended.
"Then I am willing to state your case to our council. Some of us are fond of your kind others are indifferent; yours would not be the first race to fade from existence. However, even if assistance is granted, I fear there is little we can do to help you in the long term."
"I see… So would you be willing to assist our genetic scientists find a way to stop our DNA from mutating, if your council agrees?" Lukas was somewhat mystified by the idea that this being; far more evolved than any human, didn't have a fist full of answers.
"As I say, long term solutions to your dilemma are not within our

ability. It is possible that we might find a way around human extinction, but that is a tall order my friend, and becoming something other than human hardly prevents extinction of your race."

"Other than human!?" Kartha's alarm burst from lips.

"We can alter DNA coding, even change our form, some beings live very long lives. However there is more to DNA than physical mechanics. Like all things there is a spirit influence. What is it that sets DNA in motion? A bell is silent unless something strikes it, do you understand?"

"The spark of life." Dharma's bright blue eyes seemed to exhibit that very thing.

"Yes, and it is the resonance of your friends here that enables them to do what your technology could never achieve." Thoth pointed to the hand print "ALL that you have created with your machines, your technology is no more than a pale reflection of what each of you, of what every human being can do with their minds, their being." He walked among them "YOU chose to create such things as the internet and rejected telepathic abilities, YOU created vehicles to transport yourselves rather than…"

"Projecting."

"Yourselves."

"To."

"Wherever."

"You wish to be." Several Thoths glared at them before vanishing. "You toy with DNA, it is the formula of an alchemical science YOU rejected. You are what kills yourself, you are disconnected from body, mind and souls; plugging yourselves into gadgets created as insults to nature for your amusement. And those that you rejected may well be your salvation, you are perhaps at their mercy now." He turned to the twins. "Let us see what the council has to say on the matter, I would not wish to raise your hopes though."

"You said that the sands of time had run out for us, how is this so Mr Thoth?" Arten's analytical mind remained unfulfilled.

"There are races, so ancient that time has no meaning. Amongst such beings are what we call 'the seeders' who created many races, many forms of life. They have moved worlds, cooled or heated stars in order to create conditions for life. We see their work, they however, are unseen. Undoubtedly from a far removed

dimension."
"Are they the ones who built pyramids on that terraformed world?" Mike tried to gain a perspective of alien hierarchy and influence.
"In part. That world we call Pimriya, has been influenced by a number of races. The seeders sowed Pimriya though, which is incomplete. Once it is the pyramids will be removed." Thoth felt Jack's anxiety for Caron, mingled with a multitude of questions from Mike's mind. "If you are ready to proceed I will instruct your computer, please…"
"Argo's computer is dead Sir." Lukas hesitantly informed.
"You killed Argo's mind!?"
"She sacrificed herself to save us, used her generator to fire weapons against a meteor." Mike explained.
"Then we will have to resurrect her won't we?" Thoth vanished.
"Must be a hologram or something." Kartha reasoned.
"My vote's for 'or something'." Jack muttered. "Droids returning, no life signs detected."

Stephan was somewhat surprised to find Jason Gilga working on Argo's dead brain. He might have presumed that command had kept Jason in stasis onboard, though this didn't explain white robes and certainly not why there were three Jasons. Stephan quietly stepped out of the room and was soon reassured that everything was okay, a god was taking care of things. Having then reported to the medical center he'd a very interesting conversation about the definition of insanity with Monique, who had only just finished deliberating the meaning of 'undead' having been asked by several crew members as to whether they were alive or not.

"Power fluctuation Sir." Yoto reported.
"That would be Hera." Thoth appeared on the Bridge again. "A more fitting name than 'Shom', she is more than a ship's computer, Hera is a biological entity and has her own form of consciousness. You are akin to bacteria within her body. She may take some time to fully heal."
"Fascinating, is she conscious in the sense of feelings as we are?" Mike had seen some of the experiments with AI and transplanting human brains into machines, with the catastrophic results, but this biological computer was a much earlier merging of machine and

biology; given little credit for anything other than monitoring ship's mundane functions.

"In her own way." Thoth hesitated for a moment. "Hera is a little different from other ship's brains, she was my 'pet project' as you might say."

"May I ask, is that your natural form then? Some depictions of you were ape or bird like." a line of questions shuffled forward in Jack's mind.

"My race's natural form is humanoid, though not entirely as I appear now. You and I are not so different. In some respects light years apart, in others; merely a shade away. My race did not succumb to the warlike ways of your people, we evolved with understanding, observing the realm in which we existed. It is true that we are much, much older, although the pace of life has slowed in more ways than one. My people live in what you might call the veil between third and forth dimensions, although your concept of the forth dimension is incorrect." Thoth ticked off several questions in Jack's mind.

"What's it like, where you live?" Dharma asked excitedly.

"I might ask you the same question! It is a place that resembles Earth in many ways, a continent within our realm. Other continents are devoted to different worlds and their environments, forms of life and so on. Each is like a sphere of experience to share what we have gained during our travels, living amongst other races. You will have no need of artificial apparatus there. In a moment you may be under the illusion of falling and experience nausea. It is best to keep eyes closed until you feel the sensation of your surroundings again." Thoth crossed his arms.

Lukas repeated the advice; alerting crew to sit or lay wherever they were. Moments later sight blurred, his body felt as though it were being pulled or diluted in different directions, loss of sensation in limbs, falling, spinning, yet he remained motionless as if frozen while passing through an invisible veil. A moment later, that felt like minutes, barely conscious crew groaned, hypo sprays puffed trying to restore biological balance again.

"Be still for a while, feel the grounding nature of solid surroundings." Thoth stood watching energy, that resembled

snowflakes dissipating.
"Uhh, wha was that?" Heather held her head.
"A dimensional fold. You passed through many thousands of light years by briefly entering another dimension and emerging into this one. At least that's as close as I can explain to your understanding."
"Do you always travel like this?" Jack carefully sat up, still unsure of what body part was what, hoping he'd never have to do that again.
"No, there are various portals which assist in covering great distances, we have craft which use a similar system, although it takes longer. You get used to it after a few thousand years."
"That's okay then, no problem." Lukas groaned.
"We will set down soon and you can stretch your legs, although I would ask that your crew remain in the port area for the time being. Send a delegation to the city West of here, there your case will be considered by the council." Thoth piloted Argo down through blue skies to a space port devoid of anything other than a scattering of white crystalline buildings at a forest's edge.

Recovering crew emerged into daylight, bird song and nearby trees, grateful to be in natural surroundings. For reasons Dharma would not reveal, she insisted that Yun join their delegation, as only she and Arten had been telepathically shown the way to council chambers by a vanishing Thoth, Lukas had little choice. Jack required no invite and Mike's advice might be essential. They set off, capping toward distant shimmering pyramids, Jack had no doubts as to where Caron would be, if she had any choice in the matter. Having passed over a river and meadows of wild flowers they set down at a grove of trees and shrubs on the cities outskirts, Lukas felt their approach should be more sedate and dignified than buzzing locals from above. Their pace along a natural dirt path then delayed by Dharma wanting to hear, see and smell everything, often asking Yun what birds and flowers were as she seemed to recognize them from Earth, though Dharma's main interest was butterflies, particularly the Arten and Yun variety. However, Lukas, Mike and Jack also became distracted by known predators and prey in close proximity, offering no fear or threat. Squirrels hopped around as Lukas stroked a wolf, their interactions with wildlife observed by unseen eyes. A short walk brought them to ornate gardens, pace slowed further as they admired breathtaking buildings, ancient architecture constructed of white gemstone, ornate pillars, obelisks, statues of strange and mythical creatures. They ascended steps of a building that resembled the Parthenon in Greece, though larger and not in ruins. Its outer walls bordered by columns supporting the roof. Through two columns an entrance lay ahead, offering questions of what awaited behind those doors, which suddenly burst open, a winged being striding out toward them.

"I AM THE ANGEL OF WRATH, TREMBLE BEFORE ME MORTALS, I DEMAND SACRIFICE!" Larasi boomed spreading her wings between columns.

Stunned into silence, heads turning to each other and then to Thoth now standing to their side with arms crossed, seemingly indifferent to this assault. Larasi glared at them, her left hand waving to the side for no apparent reason. She looked to the left whispering something, while mortals held their breath, not sure of what to make of the situation, surely Thoth would assure this 'angel' that they were invited guests. Larasi turned grasping the arm of another being standing behind a column, who relented, stepping out before Larasi. Her painted eyes glared wide above a veil covering nose and mouth. She inhaled deeply, filling breasts that flimsy garments could barely contain. Raising arms, white silk wings flowed down from wrists, rising up behind to her back, diamonds caressing her forehead, silk caressing and flowing over what it didn't reveal of her voluptuous body, sculpted with a degree of divine modesty.

"I AM NORAC GODDESS OF THE PIT, WHAT GIFTS WILL YOU OFFER TO APPEASE ME?"

"We… " Jack turned to Thoth who seemed more interested in a bird perched on an obelisk. "were invited by…" Jack squinted, not certain of what was before them.
"Pfft your faces" Caron howled with laughter.
"IF Mischief and Mayhem are quite finished!" Thoth raised an eyebrow at the giggling duo trying to stop each other from falling

over.

"Well big boy" Caron uncharacteristically wiggled her way down steps toward Jack. "I think you'll be the first to succumb to my will." She lifted the veil, magically transforming confusion to relief, and joy upon Jack's face.

"I am your servant oh thing of the pit." Jack's bow lifted to meet her lips.

"Oh get a room." Lukas tried to disguise his own relief and happiness to see Miss Foster safe and well, even if her cleavage wasn't uniform standard. "I wouldn't call that secure!" he muttered, sharing Caron's concerns about 'imminent fall out'.

"Oufff!" Yun, who previously stood a few feet to Arten's side, found herself bashing into him, Dharma suspiciously gazing elsewhere with a grin on her face.

"Sorry MR's Yun." Arten awkwardly tried to help her stand straight again, after falling all over him.

"I no MR's." Yun corrected, not wishing for any marital misconceptions.

"Come in, come in, you can rest and relax here during your stay." Larasi beckoned them to enter.

"One moment" Thoth raised a hand, while wearing an expression of wishing to listen to something they could not hear. "Be still, compose yourselves please. Close your eyes, do not be concerned about any sensations you may feel." Thoth waited while order returned. "Good please remain that way." He nodded toward waiting Bennus.

A degree of unease filtered through mortals as they experienced strange sensations, skin tingling, whispers or what sounded like leaves, many leaves whispering around them. Bennus drifted amongst the group, their semi translucent wings brushing over and through the party members, touching energies, minds, memories, emotions. The pair circled Dharma and Arten, paying them particular attention. Dharma flinched slightly as her mind was addressed by what seemed like a million voices whispering, slowly coming into focus as one voice, sweet, feminine, young and yet so ancient it pained to imagine just how old.

"Dhaaaarma… You are a way of things to be."

"I…" Dharma struggled to comprehend and focus on so much that seemed to be everywhere, within and beyond her. "But I have no, male… friend, I am… not wise in such ways."

"Young, so old, life teaches, we too wish your lessons."

"Not… not alone." Dharma trembled inside, all that was being asked and to deny beings such as these, to make demands took every grain of her courage. "People, there is no learning without people."

"To be a beginning?"

"No… would, would you have no others?" Dharma cringed from a moment of pain not her own. "Then you cannot ask it of me. YOU, you could teach, you could make it right."

"Then Dharma would dance?"

"Yes, well, if there is no other choice."

"There are always choices, always forms to be. We will hear your people. Speak not of this."

Dharma felt a release, steadying herself she sat on a step, unsure, frightened. Thoth informing them that he would speak to the council directly. Arten expressed concern, helping Dharma to her feet, unaware of what just transpired, although Bennus had paid him a great deal of attention. He'd heard their whispers, they had called him a guardian, of what he could not understand, nor was he meant to, yet.

Chapter Nine: Life or Death penalty

Thoth returned hours later to discover that donning of ancient fashions caused amusement amongst modern humans, who were unaware the future of their race had been debated and decided. News that they would now face the council's judgment wiped smiles and smeared doom upon faces. Thoth and Larasi guided the delegation, navigating wide avenues between buildings. Paths weaved through ornamental gardens, vine arches, passing pools and fountains. For the most part ignored by mainly humanoid inhabitants, who tended gardens, played instruments only audible to the mind or sat silently debating in small groups. Much was said, though not heard by any other than Dharma and Arten, who nodded from time to time in response to telepathic greetings. More steps led to an auditorium in which they sat on comfortable benches facing a gathering of Canatra's council; taking their seats behind a large semi circular table. Arched windows flooded the hall with light gleaming off white marble walls and mosaic floors. Thoth stood at the table telepathically communicating with twelve council members, some of whom were distinctly not human in their current form. Ulhany chaired the meeting, his turquoise head like that of a hand gliders wings, though as with Fruoisin to his left, Ulhany's body was essentially human. Fruoisin's upper body resembled that of an ant eater with a long snout, she at least had visible eyes and ears. Donshad, although humanoid was purple and no larger than a new born human, his golden slanted eyes pierced the waiting humans as he sat on the tables end, closer to delegates.

"Are you able to understand these words?" Ulhany placed his webbed hand upon a silver rod resting on the table.
"Yes." Lukas sat up.
"The device before me will translate meaning of my thoughts into your language when I touch it. Those gathered here will communicate questions through me as we are not familiar with your current language, although some of us have visited your world." Ulhany paused for a moment. "We have heard much about your primitive ways and I use no comparison to our own culture. Leadership is a matter of guidance; your leaders have used their

position to control through the ages of humanities history. Warlords, religious persecutors, governments and now corporations enslaving through fear and ignorance. It would be unwise for us to facilitate the spread of your ways to other worlds and cultures. It is for this very reason seeders have placed limits, negated only through maturing of a race. Humanity is far from mature. However, we have a dilemma in that some of you have reached an evolutionary point, that, through observation and comparison of other like species, we deem is more than adequate to meet requirements of seeders, yet too late, your people Dharma and Arten are enduring the same fate as your foolish predecessors." Ulhany sat back for a moment, before continuing, listening to comments of the council. "We feel that this new world you have taken for your own is most likely one seeders have offered as a second chance. Nothing happens without reason and we find you here asking us to do our part in this second chance. We must ask though, if we are able to assist you, where will you go from here, what are your plans?"

"Our mission brief is to report any findings to what you might call our council when we return. It's for them to decide where humanity goes from there." Lukas stood addressing the council.

"That is not acceptable slave. YOU will take responsibility for anything we are able to achieve. It is time for humans to accept responsibility for their own actions, to think for themselves as free minded beings. NOT at the whim of tyrants."

"We have our duty, but will change things if we can."

"And if not?" Ulhany waited for an answer in vain. "I offer no threat… Lukas, however you should be aware we will not tolerate humanity inflicting itself on other races. Your crimes would become our crimes as the enabler. With that said, our terms for assisting you will be that your… crew receive schooling, counseling for at least a … month, in matters of philosophy a way of life, that if you are to survive, you must embrace."

"Ethics." Thoth clarified.

"You must aspire to meet the standards that seeders have set for any race they designed. Are these conditions acceptable?" Ulhany sat back again.

"They most certainly are Sir." The thought of breaking away from humanity's old ways raised Lukas's spirits, not to mention a way

for humanity to continue existing.
"And you Dharma, are the terms now accepted." Fruoisin touched the silver rod.
"Yes." Dharma stood in her finery, white hair flowing into white silk, she gazed around nervously. "What must I do?"
"What's, err... going on?" Lukas also spoke for Arten; expressing confusion.
"There is no need for concern." Thoth crouched in front of them, speaking in hushed tones "As I said we are not able to provide you with any long term solution to your problem." He gazed toward entrance doors for a moment "But others can. Now you must remain calm, seated, please do not interrupt." Thoth stood extending a hand to Dharma. "Do not be nervous." Thoth took Dharma's trembling hand, guiding her before the council.
"And one called Arten." Ulhany's beckoning was received swiftly, Arten almost running to his Sister's side. "I am given to understand that you Dharma have negotiated with others."
"Yes Sir."
"Uhh, do not use such terms, it is something you must learn to stop." Ulhany rebuked. "You Arten, are willing to be Guardian?"
"Guardian of what Sss, Mr erm…"
"A…" Ulhany's thoughts were interrupted again "Your Sister."
"Yes of course, we look out for…"
"Very well, there are no objections to this cooperative. Your terms are agreed Dharma, are you prepared?"
"I… yes." Dharma shook her head in response to Arten's questioning.
"Then be seated for this rare and sublime occasion."
"Just a few moments Ulhany." Thoth held up a hand "Arten, please remain by my side." he turned to confused humans. "Annnd one other… Jack please join us."
"Okay." Jack strolled over "What exactly am I supposed to do?"
"You will know in a minute, do not be concerned, you have my word all will be well. Dharma, sit here, please try to relax." Thoth telekinetically brought forth an ornate crystal chair, its intricate carvings characteristic of a throne. "Be still" he knelt before her waving down murmurings from Yun and Caron.
"Please be quiet" Larasi asked an anxious Yun, Mike, Lukas and Caron. "This is what you would call sacred, so…" She turned to

gaze at auditorium doors opening "Shhh."
"It is a beautiful moment, Dharma, just allow things to be." Thoth stepped away, taking Jack and Arten with him as a Bennu glided gracefully into the auditorium.

Humans could not help but sigh and 'oh' at the being radiating a spectrum of colors through them as it passed; approaching Dharma. It was all Arten could do to stand his ground, beautiful as the creature may be, the words 'life and death' echoed in his mind, distorting to life for death. Only a combination of Jack and Thoth standing either side stopped Arten from running to Dharma's rescue. He watched nervously as the creature stopped before him.

"Your form." Its request whispered in the minds of Jack, Arten and Thoth.

Thoth held out his right palm, kneeling before Bennu, Jack and Arten following his lead, witnessing little more than a blur as Bennu's wingtips passed through their hands, gaining the vibration of their DNA. Thoth stood, gesturing that others should return to their seats, Jack using a little physical assistance to a reluctant Arten.

Dharma watched apprehensively as Bennu came to rest before her, eyes flashing to her Brother and friends, the council and then back at Bennu. Breathing became difficult, she felt great, immense power rising, her chest pained at the effort and felt like it was being ripped open until she could no longer breathe. Dharma glared at the being, heart stopping she felt peace, overwhelming peace, love to such a degree tears flowed from eyes like fountains, dripping onto silken garments. She wanted to die, or was she already there. Gaze fixed upon the Bennu it opened eyes, deep dark eyes swallowed her, Dharma's mind fell into that vastness of many dimensions, gazing upon countless worlds, an eternity of emotion, crushing sadness, tears cascaded from her eyes, she began to rise with the Phoenix. Human witnesses to emotions and energies they had never experienced before, joined her weeping at the sight of radiant mist gently flowing out of a tear drenched chest, then from her whole body, a ghostly form slowly became apparent, Dharma rising from herself. Caron held her breath, hands covering her mouth. Jack, Mike and Lukas choking back tears that Yun wiped away from her own eyes, her other hand grasping Arten's. Bennu's wings unfolded embracing Dharma's spirit, absorbing it within its own radiance. Dharma's body limply floating motionless as Bennu moved closer, wings stroked her body, now consumed in violet flames. Gradually Bennu's radiance faded into the fire shrouding Dharma's body. Caron looked away, unable to watch. Others stared in disbelief at violet flames ebbing away from a glowing form.

"It is done." Thoth whispered, lowering Dharma's body into his arms, carrying it to her friends.
"UAahh" Dharma's lungs heaved, gulping air, her hand grasping Thoth's.
"Congratulations from us all." Ulhany announced.
"Easy there." Thoth helped Dharma to her feet "Let's get you cleaned up."
"Are you okay?" Arten was the first to ask, standing whether allowed to or not.
"We thought you were… well, not with us anymore, what happened?" Caron blinked tear blurred eyes.
"I'm a bit dizzy, but we are okay." Dharma placed a hand on her stomach, looking down with a smile.
"Is it, like, inside you?" Lukas pointed.
"Yes Mr Lukas."
"Can you feel it, is it in your mind?" Jack turned as Yun caught Arten's fall.
"She's gonna have a baby you idiot." Caron swatted Jack before giving Dharma a hug.
"A baby WHAT?" Mike felt Arten had the right idea about now, best not to be conscious.
"Two souls sharing a human child." Thoth explained.
"Howww's that gonna work out?" Jack stared at Dharma's stomach.
"How aware are you of your soul Jack?" Thoth crossed his arms.
"Not a whole lot I guess."
"Well then, don't fuss." Caron defended what she thought was great news, even if the baby were born purple with green spots.

"It works just fine Jack." Thoth's eyes glowed violet for a few moments.
"How many female members of your crew?" Ulhany asked.
"What you mean we, I have to… THAT!?" Caron's idea of intimacy took on a whole new meaning.
"No Caron." Thoth reassured her, briefly glancing at Jack "We would not rob you of your moment, however, things may be other than you expected, perhaps more than you expected."
"Oh, oh err, alright then… I guess." Caron's thigh's clamped together.
"Just a moment." Lukas stepped forward. "Are you saying we have to breed, here, now?"
"Breed, is that the term you use?" Ulhany would have shook his head if physically possible.
"Well we thought you could provide a scientific solution that we can use back home… kinda thing?" Mike fished.
"That is not possible, we have part of the means to assist you here, the Bennu, have another element to add that will at least provide a permanent solution for your children. They will be a first generation and able to bare children in the usual fashion of your kind… I presume. Much is dependant on Bennu's influence in this matter. And I should warn you that these children must be isolated from your old ways, is that understood?"
"We will guard them with our lives if need be." Caron stated in no uncertain terms.
"Thank you, we have matters to arrange then." Lukas nodded to Ulhany.
"Yes thank you Sir. I use that term as a mark of respect and gratitude." Jack, shot before objections were raised.
"To answer your question I am uncertain of how many women are of child baring age in my crew, but will provide such information as soon as I can. I trust that there will be some who do not wish to… couple with anyone else though."
"Personal choice and freedom of mind is key to your survival." Ulhany advised.

--*--

Thoth surveyed a gathering of Argo's crew, whose spirits were high having been informed by Lukas that their mission was successful. Lukas raised his eyes to heaven as more adventurous crew members gradually emerged wearing suitable attire for the location and causing a stir.

"Thoth, you mentioned something about the primitive nature of our twins back in that crystalline… where was that anyway? I thought we were about to become a human soup stain on Sirius B!"
"That was Sirius B Lukas, Your ship was transported to it's centre in the same way you were transported here."
"The centre of a STAR!" Mike almost gagged.
"Sirius B is not what it may seem. Just as you might place a grain of sand within an oyster to create pearl, these gems are created through controlled orbits of a planet or moon around a star. Gravitational forces then do their work, as coal becomes diamond, so the planets matter becomes phaintonite. These spheres are often used as a terminus, meeting places for our explorers billions of light years apart.
"Fascinating!" Mike felt like he'd just set foot in scientific heaven.
"As for the twins primitive nature." Thoth considered for a moment how he might best explain. "Within us all, at least those who were designed by seeders, there is a genetic memory. Although grossly exaggerated and distorted over time and telling; so called mythical creatures are our kin, that is if your regard seeders as being our common parent. So beings such as elves, dragons; the Kahkuri and Phoenix," Thoth gestured expressing 'as you know' "minotaurs, griffins, which is what Larasi is becoming for her next adventure. Anubis is living in a town not far from here and you might consider him to be a werewolf. However, Frankenstein is very much a creature of human creation." Thoth offered a disdainful expression. "The twins might be compared to your legends of…"
"Ahem" Mike looked uncomfortable "I think there are some things the twins prefer to keep to themselves, we should respect that don't you think?"
"Is this something I should have been made aware of Sergeant?" Lukas stiffened.
"It's not of any consequence Sir, their kind have been judged enough as it is."

"That will all change soon enough." Lukas was sure to state for Thoth's ears as well.

"Can we talk privately?" Mike moved toward an area between two buildings not occupied by crew.

"I'm sure your thoughts are quite plain for our friend here to see Mike."

"Yes of course. Look the twins are kinda like grandkids to me ya know, I watched them grow up, studied their every move."

"For the Science Division, yes I'm well aware." Lukas scowled.

"They are not as aware as they might be Captain. I gave a very conservative assessment of Ashari abilities. The corporate already regard Ashari as a threat, if they knew half of what I do they.. Well." Mike glanced at Thoth. "Well as you know the twins don't exactly have much of an appetite."

"Can't say I've ever seen them in the mess hall, I presumed their shyness." Lukas raised eyebrows. "Although with diamond teeth they could make short work of the toughest steak!"

"They don't eat period." Mike confessed.

"Humans have no need of food, your consumption of flesh is quite abhorrent." Thoth commented.

"We don't? Well anyway it's hardly flesh, food is simulated these days." Lukas excused his baconic desires.

"Of course. Although the only sustenance you require is life force energy and liquids." Thoth challenged. "Your digestive organs would gradually take on other roles."

"And the twins are very adept at gathering that energy, fortunately their bone structure amplifies any absorbed energy, otherwise they might drain the life out of everyone and everything around them."

"So... so your saying that..." Lukas glanced from Mike to Thoth and back again "Kinda like vampires!?"

"Extremely kinda like." Mike's eyes widened. "They'd make kitty food out of Dracula."

"No Lukas they don't have a need to suck your blood and turn the crew into undead legions." Thoth crossed arms over his chest.

"Vampires, as you call them, have resorted to taking blood, however it's because blood is rich in life force energy... Yes there is a race of vampire like beings. No Kartha doesn't think you are an idiot and..."

"Ya, err, perhaps we could get back to questions and answers later, thanks all the same." Lukas held up a hand. "At least the twins don't have fangs and bat wings." Stress expressed itself through knuckle cracking. "DO THEY?"

"No, no bat wings, don't really need them do they." Mike shrugged.

"Think I'm having a bad dream, I'll wake up and the movie will nearly be over." Lukas shook his head.

"There are four personnel far beyond child baring age Sir" Monique stepped forward. "Natasha, Korina, Patty and myself."

"Have you children?" Thoth looked Monique up and down.

"No Sir, haven't had that pleasure, missed the chance when it was available unfortunately, still there were far too many people in the world at that time. You?"

"Oh… yes, not for quite some time though. Perhaps the elderly members of your crew would enjoy some rest and relaxation, we have spas that are quite invigorating."

"Thank you, but I'm going to be very busy I'm sure." Monique had visions of looking after more hormonally insane mothers to be than she could handle, although she could not wish for more in the late twilight years of her life.

"Take a break while you can, and you." Lukas scowled at the pair of stubborn ol coots.

"If you insist Luke, however, we must give everyone a health check before…" Monique protested.

"That won't be necessary." Thoth asserted.

"And for the last time I'm Lukas, Lukas not Luke."

"My apologies Captain, you remind me of my Brother Luke. He's still about your age and I haven't seen him for over two hundred years." Monique's familiar steely exterior began to buckle, she turned, walking back to Argo before anyone noticed.

"Hey why don't we go see some sights?" Mike, responded to the Captain's glare and pursued Monique. "I'm sure you would look stunning in one of those costumes…"

"Mike you are an old fool, I'm sure no one want's to see our wrinkles."

"AH HA!" Larasi pounced on the squabbling senior citizens, at Thoth's request. "To the gladiator pits with you!… Or would you prefer the spa of ages?" She looked from one speechless victim to the other "Free fermented juice of grape with every dip?"

"Wine you mean?" Monique frowned.
"Yes... no, it's actually extract of rueley. Tastes the same though... I think." Her head flicked back a few times gesturing behind "Do you like them? Took me three weeks to grow!"
"I'm still puzzled by your use of the term 'primitive' Thoth, seems to me these abilities make the rest of humanity look primitive." Lukas's gaze lifted from ground to meet Thoth's eyes "Do I detect a smokescreen?"
"Ah what monsters lurk in the mist of ignorance, to rend flesh from bone and bones to ash till all that remains is a naked soul, who now knows what lurks within the mist, but will any hear that soul's scream?" Thoth vanished, leaving Lukas to caste a suspicious eye upon Arten and Dharma; who wandered with Yun toward forests skirting the port.

--*--

Romance's first petals had unfolded between some crew members during their voyage and although becoming parents had hardly been on the agenda, the Captain's announcement to them all brought a sense of urgency. Crew members faced awkward questions. All felt duty bound, the situation was far from ideal, but their's was to be the generation that would continue humanity, denying a chance to bring a child into the world was unthinkable. Personnel wandered around in what they termed 'fancy dress' which added further attraction in an atmosphere of promiscuous invitation. Conversations took place in out of the way areas within the ship and surrounding parks as crew members gained courage to pop their questions.

"It's me." Lukas straightened his back before entering Kartha's quarters.
"How are things going Captain?" Kartha stood offering a nonchalant yet seductive stance, taking a cup of coffee from the simulator.
"Good, good, Maggie and Thug, Jack and Caron of course, oh and Zack..."
"And Sonya," Kartha smiled. "And you?"
"Well I..." Lukas cleared his throat as Kartha's fingers toyed with

her coffee cup "In light of our situation, I feel, not that anyone is under orders you understand…"

"Yes you said… at great length already." Kartha put her cup down, gliding toward the Captain insuring a bare leg slipped from white garments, its front and back secured only by a wide golden belt, falling to a V; accentuating her hips.

"However, I think that we could never live with ourselves if we left this duty to humanity…"

"Undone?"

"Yes, and I have admired…"

"Oh shut up." Kartha abducted his lips.

"I'm told we need to perform the honors at chambers in town, as they…"

"Practice makes perfect." Kartha's belt fell to the floor with a clink.

"Galy." Yun suggested, sitting on a log as water rippled over stones in a nearby stream.

"Gary?" Dharma questioned, stroking a squirrel, who sat by her on the grass.

"Ya Galy. Fo a boy and Isabel fo a gal."

"I like Odin, it's a very strong name." Arten defended his choice for the future fatherless child.

"Oh well, nine months to decide." Not that Dharma was taking any suggestion, but she liked the game anyway. "Aaaand what about you, your turn, what is Yun's little twiglet gonna be named?"

"Ohh, I no think about it, nobody ask me anyway. Don't liy my noodles." Yun laughed, slapping Dharma's knee.

"Oh you look very attractive in your costume, doesn't she Arten?" Dharma flicked a nut at her Brother, sitting with his back against the log.

"Yes, it, your neck is so slender, you look very graceful, a match for any Bennu." Arten couldn't believe he managed to blurt something out that didn't sound stupid; words being his second language.

"Oh… thank you, you look…" Yun, somewhat stunned, struggled to find words.

"Last call for town, please make your way to the Argo." Yoto's voice echoed through the forest.

"Oh butterfly's off to town." Dharma's smile turned to a glare at Yun, who took the hint, her hand wandering to Arten's ear, giving it a pinch.
"I no make noodles by myself." She played upon cultural stereotypes as she so often did.
"I'm not much of a cook." Arten's hand said otherwise, he stood, helping Yun to her feet.
"Ouu b…"
"No mo burrafly's." Yun pointed at Dharma as Arten led her away, hoping he wouldn't make a fool of himself and a gut full of butterflies.

--*--

Sunset graced sky with deep red and violet hues heralding the first group of prospective parents arrival in town. Excited chatter from their departure had now become an anxious silence, architecture and nature's art provided distraction for newcomers. For once Maggie and McThug were not pretending to be mortal enemies, holding each others hands as they were.

"Oh so you popped the question then!" A young grey haired man smiled at Lukas and Kartha.
"Err, yes, we, sorry do I know you?" Lukas wondered what this, and a female with him, were transforming into, although essentially human in every respect, their grey hair seemed out of place.
"It's me, me!"
"Yes it's definitely him." The young woman rolled her eyes.
"Mike!" He turned pointing at the woman "Monique, yeah ol battle… erm."
"Old what!?" Monique inflicted a look of instant death.
"Gee arguing already." Kartha smiled, what happened, no save it, we have somewhere to be." She slapped Lukas's butt.
"Awesome, what for real? Guess you two are… you know, finally?" Lukas attempted to summon the impossible dream.
"Pardon?" Monique glared.
"Girl you're only young twice don't mess it up this time." Thoth greeted the party.

"You might invoke the wrath of Dharma if you don't!" Arten grinned, Yun's head; resting against his upper arm, felt like heaven as far as he was concerned.

"I haven't really had time to consider…" Monique began to melt at the sight of Yun and Arten standing together.

"I have for a very long time." Mike moved into her space, while others moved along, granting privacy.

"Larasi and I will assist in guiding couples to their chambers, if I may have the honor?" Thoth gestured toward a low building.

"OHHH WHAT is that?" Caron's eyes were captured, along with others, by a rainbow of bright colors streaming upwards, spiraling a spectrum of energies.

"Bennus, merging, dancing in preparation, they will be present shortly." Thoth explained.

"They are gonna watch or something!?" Caron felt shy enough about this long awaited moment as it was.

"Not really, their presence is necessary and will sense when the time is right. We should go." Thoth walked on leading them into the building.

Walls displayed art of many ages, depicting ancient stories of gods, heroism and romance. Its rooms furnished with statues, couches, rugs and tables upon which fruit, musical instruments, books and other sundries rested. Thoth briefly showed them around the living room, another for their ablutions and finally a bedroom. At its centre a large very sumptuous bed seemed intimidating somehow. Surrounding this arrangement of crystals, flowers and candles rested on tables. A jug and one cup amidst the colorful displays, subdued by candlelight.

"I will say what will be said to you all," Thoth invited Caron and Jack to sit on the bed "That lust must be tempered and love triumphant, this must be a union of love. What you feel in heart and mind, what you invoke is the key to life. Balance, harmony between all things is the alpha and omega, the infinite law by which existence is governed. The law of manifestation is thus; Light" He pointed to Jack "And Love" he pointed to Caron. "In equal measure manifests Life. This is the true trinity." Thoth brought his hands together "May Love and Light be unified."

"Thank you." Caron grasped Jack's hand. "Is there anything we…"
"There is no rush, when you are ready Caron, drink a cup of the substance in this jug. That, and of course what comes naturally is all you need to do. You will experience some unusual feelings and phenomena. Nothing to worry about, they are a manifestation of love, nothing more. Now I wish you well." Thoth nodded and turned to leave.
"It was you that I saw when I nearly died on that space station wasn't it, what were you trying to say with the feather?" Jack grasped the moment before Thoth was too busy with endless tasks.
"Yes I was there when both you and Caron were about to depart your lives. I had what you might call a premonition. Such things are often abstract, but I knew we three were connected, that you and Caron were destined to meet and in some way your actions would be weighed and determine humanity's future. So I stopped your minds from releasing, a distraction from death if you like. Just enough for you to survive your ordeals. The feather represents mind, light, balanced with heart, love, as I explained. Now it is time for life," Thoth smiled and left.
"Hmm." Caron stood up inspecting flowers and crystals "Not the spontaneous, swept off my feet in the passion of the moment scenario I imagined…. Over and over, and even over again." she smirked.
"Isn't being transported back in time to an ancient world by gods, surrounded by candlelight and flowers romantic enough?" Jack stood behind, his arms resting on her waist. "Or did you want Spiderman to leap in through a window?"
"Weeeelllll." Caron giggled. "No I guess you'll do." She flicked a flower in his face, turned, embraced and kissed. "Just, you know… take it easy; going where no man has gone before."
"One small step for man…" Jack's fingers walked down her spine. "One giant leap for me!"
"Yes, I get the picture just relax." Jack brushed a finger gently over her lips.
"Should I?" Her eyes darted to the jug.
"I think so." His hand fell brushing silk covering her breast.

Caron sipped sweet juice, trying to ease nerves, feeling Jack's breath warming her neck, silk slipping from her shoulders, swallowing one last mouthful as garments fell. She almost dropped the cup as Jack's hands cupped her breasts, there was no hiding her arousal. Turning, lips caressed, candle light flickered over skin that fingers tenderly explored, his taut, covering muscles holding her soft form with a gentle strength. Soft sheets greeted Caron's back as she welcomed Jack with embracing arms, they kissed passionately, lips dancing, tongues venturing forth, his hands gliding gently over her breasts, their firm silky smooth flow interrupted only by rigid peaks that's touch brought sighs to lips and yearning to her groin. Caron's breathing quickened by sensations from her breast teased between tongue and teeth, a hand that first admired the curve of thighs, gently squeezing cheeks, then seeking permission to venture; gliding strokes upon inner thighs. She relented opening to irresistible beckoning, savoring every sensation, not knowing if his lips slowly descending kisses over her abdomen would make her scream or pass out. Caron sought to protect modesty, embarrassed by moist arousal found there, her hand soon surrendered to his lips. Moaning at pain of such pleasure, fingers grasping sheets as Jack's strong hands parted Caron's thighs, exposing her to the merciless unsought of his lips and tongue. Energies began to writhe within, threatening to explode, she gazed down to witness what drove her insane with pleasure, her breath stolen for a moment, this was it, now, it must be now, her eyes beheld a radiance, tiny flickers, flames danced over her breasts.

"Jack, UUHHH NO, No stop, Here… now." She eased his head from her flowing guilt.
"Oh geesh, are you okay?"
"Yes, its all over you as well, your on fire. Now Jack, now."
Caron's hands encouraged him, until their lips met again.
"I love you." he whispered, kissing her neck.
"And I you." Caron tried to ignore the feel of his measure and what it might do to her own.

Kissing passionately, Jack sought to align for what he could feel would be a difficult journey. Caron closed eyes tightly, feeling mounting pressure. Biting her lip, exploring with fingers, trying to ease, only to find Jack easing off. Caron flung legs around him, encouraging to do whatever it took, she would not relent. Her head shook from side to side, before a gasp escaped as he entered. A moment passed in stillness, the very air had sheens of violet drifting around them, flames flickered over her hands grasping his head, their lips met, wide, consuming each other in passion as she felt his rhythm venturing deeper and deeper. Pain eased, to discomfort, discomfort became yearning, she thrust against his rhythm with her own stride, daring to match his measure again and again. Forces of Light and Love massing, rising within them. Her fingers almost drawing blood from his back, gasping she tried to stay conscious.

"Nnnnnnnnnn" Caron's head thrashed from side to side, hands slapped the bed, attempting to release energies that threatened to blow her apart.

Jack could barely contain the inner fires, unable to stop, pleading for release, his spine ablaze with light. He felt it, almost there, almost. Caron's body contorted, her back arching up to him, eyes sprang open, mouth gaping awaiting. She screamed, Jack gritted teeth as a climax ripped through them both, shrieking along spines inciting convulsions of breathless, paralyzing ecstasy. Minutes of silence passed before Jack finally collapsed to her side.

"That was… out of this world!" Caron cuddled up to her panting lover.
"Damn right it was, I've never experienced an orgasm I thought would kill me before." he stroked her hair.
"I wonder if your little sailors found a ship to board?" Caron twiddled with Jack's chest hair, taking a quick peak at the invading article between his legs.
"Yeeessssss." a whisper echoed through their minds.
"Erm… thanks you." Caron's eyes scanned the room, not really expecting to see anything.

Chapter Ten: A precious cargo

A month extended to seven weeks; the time it took for some couples to learn differences between love and lust, or simply for romance to blossom; love being the spark that ignited Bennu's flames. In the meantime some of nature's secrets were revealed to Argo's crew. Thoth spent much time with the twins, who were secretive about their lessons. Arten became increasingly aware of what it meant to be a guardian, Thoth groomed him for leadership. Although every minute away from Yun pained him, Arten made up for it after school, fussing over her. They all learnt much, and for most the donning of suits brought with it sadness, a longing to remain in peace, but this was not their world. At least the prospect of returning again with others from Ashari cheered their parting.

"This crystal will act as a key to unlock Hera's mind." Thoth stood with a small group as the last crew members boarded. "Within Hera's mind is a crystal matrix that contains information you need to locate us again. Just place it in any of Hera's ports. Guard it well, your computers are wiped bare of anything pertaining to your trip here, Yes Mike the shuttle's too." Thoth handed Lukas what appeared to be a quartz crystal, though with barely visible ridges and shapes that resembled microchips when sunlight caught its surface. "And for the guardian I give this." He placed a necklace around Arten's neck, furnishing a deep red gem. "For the butterfly queen." Dharma smiled lowering her head to receive her crystal, unlike Arten's it was an almost luminous violet/electric blue. "Ah you will know their nature in time I'm sure."
"Thank you, it's beautiful." Dharma admired the pendant.
"And for you Caron." Thoth held out both hands, in which gradually manifested a tome, golden, glimmering in the sunlight.
"The Book of Life. Also to be guarded well."
"Oh, oh my, its… REAL! It's a treasure beyond compare, it, it weighs a ton!" Her arms shot down as Caron received the book, which then floated under Arten's influence.
"Thank you for everything, sorry humanity let you down, we won't again." Lukas shook Thoth's hand.
"Thank you Prince amongst men." Caron kissed his cheek, her hug

expressed more of a soul felt gratitude.

"Oh here you are." Larasi appeared "Do have a pleasant faltering step won't you." she returned puzzled expressions.

"Trip." Thoth felt the need to adopt another teaching role, although Larasi never completely got anything right, other than her playful loving heart.

"Can we take her home?" Monique grinned.

"I don't think we have any room in our circus for another member. GET ON BOARD YOU TWO" Lukas yelled at Zack and Sonya who screamed her way passed, pursued by Zack impersonating a five year old monster. "Erm, I suspect those aren't regulation flowers Corporal," he stopped Yun in her tracks as she tried to sheepishly hide behind Arten, who then shrugged removing flowers from her hair, that she'd habitually worn for weeks. "Your work I presume?" Lukas looked accusingly at Larasi.

"Who?" Larasi looked behind herself discovering no one else to blame. "ME!"

"Personal choice," Thoth reminded.

"Actually they suit you. However, I'm not sure how I'm going to explain a Chinese PIXIE to Admiral Carter when we get home!" Lukas glared at Yun's pointed ears.

"I eat magic noodle." Yun invoked her 'I didn't do it' little girl look.

"I have no desire to hear details of your sex life." Lukas turned back to Thoth "Well before I discover anymore monsters in the mist we had better go, thanks you so much again."

"Take care of your children and may love be your guide." Thoth bowed.

"Good purchase." Larasi waved with her tail, that took her two weeks to grow.

--*--

Overcoming nausea was about the only eventful occurrence on their voyage home. Lukas struggled to maintain discipline amongst his born again flower power crew who most certainly wanted to make love not war. Although if the howls and screams were anything to go by there wasn't much difference. Each shift change started with the same briefing, day after day a story was told that didn't include Pimriya, Kahkuri, gold, pyramids or sand castles for that matter. No one was to reveal that part of their journey. Lukas felt confident that his crew, or clan as McThug had aptly termed them, would betray their secret. They had indeed become a fiercely loyal family, one that approached Mars with reluctance.

Earth did not roar, there was no brass band. The saviors of humanity were greeted by military brass and corporation gold. Very self important people rarely seen and for the most part unknown shook the crews hands, patted backs and congratulated them on a mission, most thought these expendables, would never return from. Humanity's sickness left a dank odor in the air. Amidst initial demands for interviews that would never be released to the media, debriefings, and the tragic news of another major eruption on Earth that had destroyed a stasis station, women were led away for 'health checks', as were formally elderly members of the crew. Private meetings took place discussing the implications, the potentials, not so much for humanity, but an ageing hierarchy of greed.

Six days passed during which Argo's crew prepared for a rescue mission to save whatever souls survived the earthquake in Africa. Six days of excuses as to why the men could not visit their partners confined deep within the Mars research facility; built deep into a huge crater, few ever accessed its lower levels and the entire instillation was shielded from psychic probing. Any thoughts Dharma may have sent were scrambled, Arten could not even reach the minds of station personnel. He'd probed the minds of new crew members, all from Earth satellite stations, recently brought out of stasis and oblivious to events of the past two hundred years. One exception was a science officer from the Mars facility, Arten detected anxiety, she was hiding something, though oddly he could not focus on what. Finally Admiral Carter summoned Lukas for a briefing at Earth moon's military station.

"Sit, Lukas." Admiral Terrance Carter gestured to a seat facing his desk "I must apologize for the confusion and poor treatment of your crew, after all you have achieved you should be sitting in my chair. Things will be set right as the dust settles I'm sure.

However, as your ship is currently the only vessel with a gravity wave generating system, we must call upon you, and the experience of your crew, to venture again for assistance…"

"You want us to go back… already!?" Lukas frowned in disbelief.

"Well as your systems were able to provide such scant data," Terrance eyed him suspiciously "we can only rely on your experience."

"I'm not confident that we can repeat that journey Sir, we were almost ripped apart by forces we don't fully understand and it was that which sent us to who knows where, such a phenomena may not be achievable again."

"We have a duty to try Captain, to find a means, a definable route. You achieved much but it would seem none of it benefits more than female members of your crew. So we want you to return with five hundred stasis pods, obviously occupied by women of child baring age."

"Five hundred! Sir you… perhaps you have not been fully informed, conception still requires intimacy, there are no test tube scientific implant methods, there has to be love between the guys and girls ya know."

"Your crew's hippy attitudes have been reported to me Lukas, but I'm willing to overlook that lapse in professional standards. I'm certain your young marines will be able to sow a few more seeds for the sake of humanity and," Terrance grinned "their personal score sheets. Would go myself but the damn corporate wouldn't let me have any fun."

"My men will at least be able to visit their partners before we set out?" Lukas felt sickened by the Admiral's attitude, he knew better than to speak his own mind though.

"I doubt that will be possible, Captain, the facility is strictly off limits to anyone without the highest security clearance due to the nature of research in some areas. And the women are under constant observation; they may reveal some answers yet. You know these science nerds, everything has to be controlled, confined and measured."

"With respect Sir, damn the nerds we have some rights…"

"Captain have you forgotten the mess we are in? You are lucky to be a survivor, and I would remind you that there are other officers who have survived and would gladly take your place."

"Yes Sir." Lukas had heard enough, any further response would be on autopilot.
"Your cargo will be arriving soon from Mars stasis two and four, the shuttle returning you to Mars will replace the one you lost. Is there anything else you require for this mission?"
"I believe damaged equipment has been replaced, although we have been on standby for a week so I will need to run an audit."
"The research facility should be able to supply almost anything required. Good luck Captain that will be all." Carter dismissed Lukas with an arrogant wave.

--*--

Lukas piloted the shuttle on it's return journey to Argo, dismissing it's assigned pilot, wishing to be alone with his thoughts, dark thoughts. He would have told Admiral Carter to stick his orders where the sun don't shine, but then he'd be powerless to do anything about the crew's situation, what could he do though, half his crew locked away beyond reach including Mike; the one person who might have some ideas, knowing the facility as he did. Arten could do nothing. How could he tell the crew of this, they would lynch him. Lukas docked in Argo's hanger bay with a very troubled mind and made straight for the Conference Room, ordering key personnel to meet him there as he strided along corridors with a mean look on his face.

"So those are our orders." Lukas waited for a reaction from Jack, Arten, Lieutenants; Yoto, Craig, Grant, Anwar.
"Good luck Captain, I'm going nowhere without Rhianna." Grant affectively resigned.
"My first pointless reaction Grant, we must stick together."
"I'm all for returning to Paradise but not without the girls." Craig sat down as if to say he wasn't going anywhere either.
"And our children." Anwar added.
"We have to get them out Lukas, I don't trust these bastards." Jack scowled.
"Arten?" Lukas turned to the silent guardian "Anything to add?" He stepped away as the back of a chair crumbled in Arten's hand." Wow, okay kid, take it easy, calm down."

"And you Captain, what are your thoughts?" Yoto knew they were the only ones that really counted.

"I agree with Jack, we have to release them and get the hell out of here, beyond that I really don't know, just put some space between the corporation and us. Right now we don't have much time. I have a few ideas, but first off we have outsiders to deal with. Arten you need to think clearly now, we need you…"

"They are innocent of this, there is one who hides something I don't know what, the Doctor, Mrs Clair."

"The ones I met are okay Captain, no anal corporate stooges." Anwar shared.

"Alright, Yoto, Craig prepare Argo for emergency take off, but keep it discrete. Grant, prep all auxiliary craft, for now it's just a pre-mission test.. Anwar get your men armed and ready I doubt they are gonna let us go without a fight. Jack I'll call new crew here for a briefing, act like you're a medic." Lukas punched a code into Jack's suit controls altering personnel status; colors and bands on his left arm.

"Give them a sedative, Mahindra will assist he's now a field medic, or herbalist at any rate… What are you grinning at Grant?"

"Nothing Sir, just some of us have smoked a few of his remedies."

"I'll be sure to underline sedated not stoned." Lukas lingered a stare at Grant and Anwar whose smirks admitted guilt. "Until our new friends are incapacitated this is all a drill. Arten, with me, we have someone to drill. Get to it people."

--*--

"So Doctor, I have a few questions." Lukas gestured for her to take a seat in the medical centre as Mahindra removed various items.

"Yes Sir." Clair eyed Arten nervously aware of his abilities, or at least some of them.

"I need them fast Clair, what's going on in your den out there?"

"I," she looked from Lukas to Arten, both glaring at her "I've only worked there a month, scarcely know my way around."

"What are you doing to them?" Arten leant forward.

"I don't know honestly… I don't think it's entirely ethical though."

"What do you mean EXACTLY?" Lukas put a hand on Arten's shoulder as if he were trying to calm a mad dog marine.

"I don't have security clearance for their level, I'm not a corporate ass kisser, all I know is that some sinister old farts were visiting and getting heavy with Professor Millard. They wanted results no matter what… Look I'm glad to be out of there, I would have said something, but I don't have evidence of anything."
"Okay Doctor, so how do we get down there?" Lukas sat on the edge of an examination table.
"You can't."
"I wouldn't count on it." He thought for a moment "So whose side are you on sister?"
"I'm certainly not on their side Sir."
"She's telling the truth Mr Lukas." Arten answered the Captain's questioning glance in his direction.
"You willing to help us?"
"Can't see what I can do, but yes if my skills are needed."
"Okay, you and Arten will enter the facility with a group of marines to procure equipment. Do what you can to assist him."
"With what aim?" Clair looked apprehensively at them both.
"Arten will be able to assess what we can do once he's not hampered by the psychic shielding." Lukas gestured toward the hatch, encouraging more haste and less doubt.

Assembling a squad, who were ready to rip the facility apart on hearing the news, Lukas put his plan into action, a plan immediately delayed. The squad waited pensively in a freight shuttle for twenty five minutes, while throughout Argo crew prepared to meet any resistance. Lukas verbally shredded the depot's duty security officer, stating they had a mission to get on with and if he didn't get his act in gear Argo would use him for target practice. With a grudging arrogance officer Simpson permitted entry. Fortunately only Simpson met Wayne and Tyler at the maintenance depot, he seemed annoyed to be dealing with 'space monkeys' asking for a bunch of junk he'd have to find. Simpson's labors were short lived; leaving him unconscious. Wayne gave the all clear, a cargo of marines off loaded procuring items not included on their list, such as sonic grenades.

"Picking anything up Arten?" Anwar, attached grenades to his utility belt.

"Too many minds, I can't find Dharma or Yun, none of them."
"They are probably unconscious, and definitely so if any are like you." Clair advised.
"You and the Doc sniff around, if they see us marching through Sterileville they'll know something ain't right. Sure you're okay with that kid?" Anwar wasn't at all sure about sending a civilian into what could become a very dangerous situation, especially not a gentle soul like Arten.
"Be sure you are ready Mr Anwar." Arten turned toward terminal access doors with a far from gentle glint in his eyes.

"Who is this?" A somewhat alarmed administrator stopped Clair and Arten attempting to navigate corridors of the first level, without attracting attention.
"He's a patient, need to get him treated." Clair's eyes signaled what she meant by 'treatment'.
"I'll take him down." Gustaf motioned to take Arten's arm.
"Not without her, no, I won't." Arten backed away.
"Alright, alright." Gustaf had no intention of squabbling with some freak show psychic and led them to an elevator, his DNA scanned they descended three levels "Okay this way." he huffed, exiting the elevator and managing a few paces "UGgghh" Gustaf held his throat.
"I strongly suggest you tell us where the Argo women are being held before my friend here crushes more than your throat." Clair knelt by a collapsed administrator, who nodded.
"Lev… level five" Gustaf gasped.
"Okay get us down there." Clair pointed to the elevator.
"I don't have clearance, you'll get nowhere." Gustaf passed out.
"Wait here." Arten dragged him into a room and headed back to the elevator; forcing doors open, he peered down a shaft.
"Now what? I'm not climbing down there!" Clair protested "Oww, AHhh I don't like heights." She clung to Arten, burying her face in his shoulder as they floated down.
"Report." Anwar's voice hissed.
"I will let you know when supplies are ready Lieutenant." Arten replied, hovering at level five doors.
"Now what?" Clair clung even tighter to Arten who failed to open doors with one hand.

"Be quiet for a moment." Arten placed his palm against the door, closing eyes.
"Your… You… How can…" Clair couldn't believe what she saw; metal turning to sludge in Arten's hand, creating a hole in the door.
"Ouukay." She thumped down on the floor after squeezing through. "Surprised we haven't set any alarms off yet."
"If no one can get in what's the point in having alarms. Wait here." Arten peered into an empty room.

Opening door after door they found nothing but empty accommodation or equipment storage, ducking into one room at the sound of voices approaching from another corridor. Arten gained nothing in their current thoughts that would aid his search, which he resumed. Turning into another corridor he sensed Dharma, her presence was close..

"What are you doing down here marine?" A security officer reached for his sidearm, only to find himself hurling along the corridor, hitting a wall at its end.
"Think you killed him!" Clair watched the officer slide down, leaving a trail of blood.
"I didn't think… Our suits protect us from impacts like that." Arten felt numb, as if the taking of a life had taken something from him.
"Well these guys aren't expecting your kinda trouble. Lets get on with it, we don't have time to clear up that mess." Clair grasped his arm, shaking Arten into life, pulling his fixed gaze away.
"Dharma is close, I can feel her." He paused by several doors, finally entering one brightly lit examination lab, making straight for an attendant leaning over a bed.

"Who…?" Was all Phaedra could say before Arten's hand covered her mouth, a pointless action as the dead guard's body had already been found.
"What have you done to Dharma?" Arten growled, looking down at tubes and sensors invading her body.
"Stand away." Guards entered, aiming pulse rifles at Arten's head.

Arten released the attendant, turning slowly to three officers standing by the door. He tensed, head tilting slightly to one side in a gesture of 'who do you think you're kidding?'. One guard flew upward; head smashing against the ceiling, blood gushing from his nose just as two more were thrown against each other; heads butting, all landing in a heap. Turning back he found Phaedra cowering in a corner, while Clair moved to examine Dharma. More security personnel burst in, before they could assess what was going on Arten launched at them and several pulse beams hit him. He stood motionless, they fired again and again, blasting red laser shots at him as if in slow motion. Arten felt heat throbbing on his chest, watching a surreal scene as pulse beams hit an invisible shell around him, knowing now what Thoth's crystal gift was for. He gazed up at men with hatred in their eyes, their yelling silent to his ears, arms jerking back from constant firing recoil. He gazed over at his Sister's defiled body, down to Clair bleeding out on the floor, her shoulder ripped open. Despite the suits protection, it could only take one or two hits in the same place from such weapons, a third had taken her down. Arten gazed back at the frenzied guards and became the monster in Thoth's primordial mist. Seconds later blood soaked lacerated bodies lay dead and dieing. He turned to Phaedra.

"NO, NO, PLEASE!" Terror in her eyes fixed upon diamond fangs set within a blood stained face approaching with menace.
"Arten what's going on?" Anwar stared at red alarm lights blinking from walls.
"Destroy them." The tip of a razor sharp claw touched communication controls on Arten's forearm.
"Arten, what is going on?... ARTEN." Anwar's question unanswered he signaled for marines to secure level one.
"YOU." Arten's mind floated a sobbing Phaedra from her crouched position, while she attempted to grasp worktops in vain.
"If they die so do you." He released, Phaedra dropped and scrambled to stand up, aided by a hand full of lethal claws.
"No, she, let me." Phaedra's trembling hand's eased his grasp of her uniform and made quick work of disabling instruments, removing sensors and trying to bring Dharma around. "It will take a little while." She sobbed, praying no one would attempt a rescue and infuriate the thing watching her. "Can you?" Phaedra pointed

to an empty examination table as she knelt by Clair.
"Move." Arten lifted Clair, floating her to the table. "Will she live?"
"Yes, if I have anything to do with it. Please just…" She gestured for him to back away.

Arten made for the door, moving swiftly along a corridor feeling vibration of an alpha droid clanking along a nearby corridor. He waited, back against a wall, listening to guards checking each room, progressing along another corridor behind and to his right, the alpha droid ahead of them ready to deal with intruders. Arten concentrated, the droid slowed, straining to walk forward, prompting comments from guards about junk robots. They drew closer, just around the corner, Arten's sudden cessation of telekinetic force launched the droid forward smashing into a wall under it's own force, knocked off its feet by the impact. Guards froze as the droid attempted to stand again. Seconds later guards fell in a frenzy of claws, some thrown at the droid who couldn't lock targeting systems on the blur amidst a decreasing number of guards. Lethal talons sliced through flesh and bone, powered by a guardian's fury, a whirlwind of merciless revenge. Finally Arten picked up a pulse rifle and blasted at the encumbered droid. Proceeding on he left bloody bodies, groaning, broken and barely conscious.

One, amongst a dozen medical staff and scientists pointed a weapon at Arten as he burst into the main lab of that section. The guardian waited for him to fire, his mind then wrenching the weapon out of hands, hurling it across lab tables and instruments. Arten glared at paralyzed empty scientific shells of former human beings, fear now at least some sort of feeling in their hearts. Surveying the lab he saw Mike laid out, blood being siphoned from his arm.

"Arten…?" Mike's weak voice questioned, his sight blurred
"Arten, help… me." he pleaded to the one who could barely control his rage.
"Release him." Arten spat between fangs, blood dripping from his suit. "Return his blood." he moved to Mike's side, watching for

any movement while one medic helped to revive Sergeant Palmer.
"Are you okay Mr Mike?"
"Yes, thank you, the others, you must find them." Mike tried to sit up, blood now pumping back into his veins.
"Who wishes to live?" Arten asked of the fearful staff, who replied with various affirmatives, unsure if they were just being toyed with. "Release our crew and don't attempt anything foolish, I am in no mood for games."
"I wouldn't trust them Arten." Mike snatched a hypo spray, from the physician, setting it to dose himself with stimulant.
"There are marines on level one, you get past me and they will give you a taste of Mars air. You understand?" Arten's claws glinted.
"Yes, we'll attend to your crew immediately." The previous weapon wielder assured him.
"Go, go find your Sister and Yun, I'll be okay in a few minutes, go on." Mike waved him away.
"I'll take you to them." Mike's temporary physician offered.
"Lead on then, take me to Yun."

"Where am I?" Dharma began to stir.
"Just rest for a minute." Phaedra puffed a few more stimulants into Dharma neck, before turning back to Clair. "I need to get you into surgery." she shook her head, barely able to stop the bleeding with so few instruments at hand.
"What happened?" Dharma sat up, still drowsy.
"Your friend happened, looked like you, well he did at first."
"Arten? Oh, my, is she okay?" Dharma eased off her bed, reaching to stroke Clair's hair.
"I hope so, my life depends on it. Look your things are in the cabinet over there, sooner you're out of here the better." Phaedra didn't want to deal with another crazed Ashari.
"Arten wouldn't do this." Dharma stood naked, placing Thoth's gift around her neck before slipping into the viro suit.
"I guess he didn't have much choice. Oh God." Phaedra threw more fragments of bone and tissue into a steel bowl. "I'm not a surgeon, this is worse than I thought." Blood smeared over her cheek from a hand trying to wipe away tears.
"Maybe I can get some help?" Dharma stood by Phaedra, looking

over Clair.

"There's a war going on out there girl, you... well I guess you'd better stay here. NO don't touch that please." Phaedra caught Dharma's hand hovering over Clair's wound.

"I... have to." Dharma submitted to the involuntary movement of her arm, eyes flickering violet, she felt a pulsing between breasts and stirring energy from her abdomen.

"What are you doing?" Phaedra stepped back, eyes fixed on golden light glowing around Dharma's hand. "Oh gees!" she watched as tiny electric blue flashes knitted tissue and bones together like divine needles, faster than any device could achieve. "I think you were sent from Heaven and the other one from Hell." She could see new skin forming through a golden haze.

Anwar's squad made short work of level one's security, now they waited for a response from at least fifty marines, stationed at or near the facility. Their stasis pods deactivating when alarms were triggered. Anwar had no solid intel on the barracks location, where to expect an attack from, or when. He continued to search a console for information while Wayne and McThug questioned prisoners.

"Can you disarm the meteor cannons?" Lukas asked, wishing he were there to sort things out for himself.

"Can't do shit at the moment Sir, need security clearance to order coffee around here and I don't trust any of this filth anywhere near systems."

"You must find Arten and the crew..."

"Hang on Captain. Yes?" Anwar hoped Rick had something to offer.

"Crew are down at level five, elevator controls won't respond though. You want us to drag one of the staff down there?"

"Wait up. Captain did you hear that?"

"Yes, hold your position, reinforcements on the way, disable security barriers anyway you see fit."

"Will do Captain." Anwar grabbed his rifle, gesturing for Rick and Tyler to follow. "Arten please report...Dammit." He blasted several security scanners approaching the main facility exit, moving on toward airlock hatches.

"He damage controls, not pily dow here."
"YUN, Oh shit it's good to hear your voice, what's going on?" Anwar's expression flooded with relief.
"We okay, gelling noodles togela, we be up in tweny minute. Alen… he upsey, he… I see you soon."
"Yeah… okay." Anwar, sensed from Yun's awkward conversation that not all was good news. "Right lets get this thing open. He ripped a panel off the wall looking for a way to bypass airlock hatch controls.
"That won't be necessary." two arms revealed themselves from behind a security desk, followed by a guard hoping to save the rest of his skin.

It wasn't long before another ten marines entered the facility. Argo lifted off, two pairs of auxiliary pulse cannons rose from her upper hull, turning toward facility meteor defenses and blowing cannons to pieces with a few precautionary shots. Yoto kept a close eye on sensor readings, watching for any activity that might require more firepower.

Arten gradually returned to normal, his fury subsiding, claws and fangs retracted although mental scars on a normally peaceful mind didn't. Glad and surprised to find Clair fit and well, he nearly crushed Dharma to death with a hug the moment they set blue eyes on each other. The women soon organized and armed themselves. Mike and other men, who's youth had been restored, joined them. There was little time for tearful reunions, Phaedra waited by elevator controls ready to send groups up to level one.

"There's my useless sack of…" Maggie leapt on McThug who spun around in circles with her legs and arms wrapped around him.

Others emerging from the elevator were told to save it for later and assemble by the main hatch. Anwar's squad grew anxious, it seemed like forever; waiting for one elevator load after another and yet still no sign of instillation defenses. Boarding one of Argo's shuttles eased tensions, crew were safe even if marines should show up. Just a few more personnel to rise from facility depths and they could all get out of there.

"That everyone?" Mike stood with Arten, Dharma, Yun and Natasha.
"Yep by my count." Natasha, like Mike; now with the appearance of a twenty one year old, stepped into the elevator.
"Yes that's all of you." Phaedra stared at the floor, guilt averting eye contact. "I'm sorry for what they, we have done, we don't all have a choice. I thought the prospect of children would be cause for rejoicing... Anyway, good luck to you."
"Yes, good luck to you too." Dharma joined Natasha.
"Take me with you… please, please, anything's but this." Phaedra, barely five feet tall, glanced up at them one by one, hoping someone might understand.
"Your kidding right!?" Mike glared at her.
"Uhh, nn…" Phaedra flinched as Arten grabbed her arm.
"Redeem yourself." he shoved her into the elevator.

"Incoming." Yoto alerted "A hawk and two ravens, ETA forty seconds Captain."
"Fire." Lukas had no second thoughts, cannons lit Martian terrain with blue flashes before a fireball smashed into its surface.

Chunks of a hawk's fuselage spinning, crashing across red desert landscape. A raven's cannons exploded either side of a direct hit from Argo's huge pulse cannons vaporizing the interceptor. Red dust and rock bloomed up from a second raven's blistering cannons sweeping across Argo's hull with little affect other than a glancing blow to her engine ports. The raven maneuvering away too fast for Argo's auxiliary cannons to lock on target.

"Get that damn thing outta my sky." Lukas barked as the raven turned for another run and Argo's thrusters kicked in.
"We got company here" Anwar yelled over the sound of weapons discharging and a reception area turning into a scrap yard.

Four hovering sonic grenades achieved nothing other than knocking out Phaedra in the elevator and nearby prisoners: helmets protected everyone else. McThug continued to decimate a corridor with two pulse rifles, pinning down marines at it's far end, Tyler and Wayne joining him though not much could be seen through ceiling panels crashing down, sparks and small fires. An occasional red beam fired in return doing little to further progress of instillation defense forces. The raven's pilot fired at nothing but red dust kicked up by Argo's thrusters. Emerging from the cloud she did not expect to find two of Argo's ravens on her tail. Fortunately having the sense to eject before her interceptor disintegrated.

"Nice try." Zack watched interceptor fragments impacting Mars surface. "Anything else you want trashed Captain?"
"Just get your asses back here, I don't plan on sticking around for an encore."

"Clear, get yourselves to the airlock fast." Anwar signaled to the last group of liberated elevator dwellers. "Whatcha got there kid?"
"A little memento of our visit," Arten walked by with an unconscious Phaedra over his shoulder.
"Ya noodle soup." Yun suggested.
"Okay, relay guys, Wayne…" Anwar orders cut as McThug stumbled back, collapsing from a volley of shots to his stomach.
"Shit, Rick, Konrad, get him to the shuttle. Ferret, cover Wayne and Tyler."

Leaving Dharma, Clair and Mike to board with Phaedra, Yun and Arten assisted McThug. Rick and Konrad positioning to cover the retreat of others. Wayne and Tyler ran back to take Anwar and Ferret's position. So it went on, relaying back along a wide passage with its various security points, between airlock and reception area. Opposing marines progressing along a corridor toward them despite growing casualties. Arten crouched by Yun acting as snipers, a constant stream of laser fire flashing back and forth. Anwar and Ferret made a final run for it, hit several times they stumbled, diving into the first security area either side of the hatch, which now was in clear line of enemy sight.

"Now what?" Tyler sat with his back to a desk. "Go for the hatch and get fried!"
"It will take fifteen to twenty seconds to open that and get in

there." Anwar flinched at sniper shots from the reception area.
"Wha?" Yun refused to release her rifle to Arten.
"You just get in there when I say." Arten gave her a stern look, one that Yun had never seen before.
"You play helo enough today."
"Trust me."
"Noo I no leh you geh flied."
"You protect our baby." Arten snatched her rifle away, mimicking McThug he stood with two rifles, blasting away, moving toward a marine reception.
"Kid, get, crap, get to the airlock, I'll cover." Anwar opened fire.

Arten's chest felt heat again as laser shots were absorbed by his shield. A terrified security officer cursed airlock controls for being so slow, every second felt like an hour as Saraven stood vulnerable at the hatch, Arten blasted anything that moved with both mind and pulse rifles, forcing marines to change from offensive fire to defensive cover. Finally the hatch opened, Saraven its first occupant, Wayne grabbed a protesting Yun, dragging her in followed by others.

"He's too far away." Anwar diving in last. "Open the outer hatch." he hardly had to instruct Saraven who'd been playing door man for the past twenty minutes. "On board." Anwar ordered.
"No, I way fo Alen."
"GET ON THE SHUTTLE." Anwar grabbed Yun.
"No I lip you eyes out." Yun demonstrated the oriental art of kicking, punching and screaming, having little affect on a viro suit.
"Take me with you and I'll wait as long as I can." Saraven offered.
"Okay." Anwar agreed.
"Cowshi." Yun activated titan mode and threw Anwar into the shuttle. "Have nice tlip." the door closed before Anwar could pick himself up.

Marines summoned reinforcements; two alpha droids marched through reception striding toward Arten, lasers blistering short bursts from each arm. Marines ceased fire, waiting for droids to return after wreaking carnage, it certainly sounded like the world was ending in the passage. Yun felt she was dieing more with each passing second, hearing the destruction, metal screeching against metal, heavy firepower ripping everything apart, ceiling and wall panels crashing down. Then silence. Marines stood up from their cover, cautiously moving toward positions to gain a line of sight along the passage. A carcass screeched along the floor into reception, slamming against a wall, followed by its head.

"Holy Mother of God." Tyler muttered as Yun boarded the shuttle, while others backed away from the creature holding her hand.

Chapter Eleven: In the blink of an eye

"Engine port malfunction." Hera reported in response to the Captain's command for maximum velocity.
"Great, that's all we need! Hera, detail malfunction." Lukas felt a headache coming on.
"External damage to section five, reducing capacity by fifteen percent. Structural integrity holding.
"Plot course for Sarfayon system wave, let's get the Ashari out of harms way." Lukas ordered as Mars fell away behind Argo.
"That will take us to the far side of the sun and pass close to Earth, Captain." Yoto warned, concerned about lunar station's military port.
"Anything on the scanners?"
"Not yet Sir." Yoto's gaze fixed at Earth and it's moon on Kartha's console display, waiting for any sign of movement.
"Lunar station has a small fleet, let's hope they don't have anyone to fly them." Lukas shifted apprehensively in his seat.
"Hope you boys have been behaving." Kartha planted a quick kiss on Lukas's cheek, before her she and Heather took their usual stations.
"Ahhh nice to see some butt on the Bridge." Lukas grinned.

"Fine job yeh done there lass" McThug peered down at a scorched, torn suit, hardly believing his stomach was back in one piece.
"Yes!" Monique seemed fixated on what was blood and guts
"Have you ever thought about being a nurse Dharma?"
"Ya okay." Dharma found the prospect exciting "We already have two more though." she looked back at Clair and Phaedra.
"Oh I think we are going to have our hands VERY full soon enough!" Clair smiled.
"A ship full of babies." Phaedra spoke quietly, trying to integrate, but feeling very much an outsider: condemned by everyone else.
"I need to get this bird turned around people." Grant prompted remaining passengers to get off the shuttle.
"Okay Phaedra and Saraven with me, you need to get suited up." Mike gestured for them to follow.
"Yes an I need to get you outta yours." Maggie wiggled

suggestively at McThug.

With no time to waste, crew members returned to their usual duties. Pilots sat tensely waiting in cockpits for any launch commands. Engineers closely monitored excessive vibration coming from one engine port hit during the interceptor attack. Medical personnel tended to minor injuries sustained by marines. Jack, Caron, Yun and Dharma tended to Arten, who sat in Yun's quarters, silent, troubled. They tried to convince him that the monsters face was worn by the corporate, not he. As Yun repeatedly pointed out; Arten was the hero, their savior. Jack's brief and blurred glimpse of something when Dharma smiled a little too broadly, after they didn't impact on Sirius B, now revealed itself as she bared her own fangs; reminding Arten he was not the only one capable of tapping into their worlds primitive gifts. Yun finally asked for privacy to clean blood from her man's body and replace his wrecked suit. Tension grew on the Bridge as Argo passed Earth and its moon, ignoring threats from Admiral Carter to return their precious cargo, or the Science Division would obtain all the DNA they needed from frozen carcasses in space.

"Two, two eagles Sir." Kartha alerted.
"Crap, can't we get anything more from engines? We have to catch a wave before they catch us."
"No Sir, if we push our luck we could rip the ports apart and be in deeper trouble." Heather reminded.
"ETA seven minutes Sir." Kartha watched two blips closing in on them. "Recommend offensive action Captain, hit them before they hit us."
"No, hold our course." Lukas's mind looked beyond the approaching sun, thoughtfully distracted.
"Alls well with…" Mike entered.
"Take a seat Mike. How many bandits Kartha?"
"Still two Sir."
"Hmm, okay. Visual." Lukas stared at two eagle class ships side by side.
"Stand down Griffin." Lieutenant Sahra Garson's face appeared on the Bridge's main screen.
"Or what Lieutenant, you kill humanity's last hope?" Lukas

donned an expression of 'your dealing with an old dog little yapper'.

"Or I'll take out your engines and drag your ass back to face the music." 'Little yapper' snapped back.

"Think we'll take our chances if it's all the same to you."

"Admiral Carter is offering you one last chance, you and your crew are offered an amnesty, surrender now or I'll shoot you myself."

"Yeah let's all go back and be corporate lab rats. You tell Carter to back off and maybe we will return with answers some day."

"Your funeral." Sahra gestured for the Saber to fire.

"They're firing Captain… just warning shots." Kartha advised.

"Okay, okay, we're outnumbered and can't outrun them." Lukas nudged Mike, sitting to his left. "I accept your terms Lieutenant Garson. Bring her to a stop Ensign Martha."

"Set your course for the lunar Station Captain." Sahra ordered, with a face that would sour milk, or her other pastime of making men impotent.

"The reason you caught us is that we have damaged engine ports Lieutenant. We either need to fix them or transfer our crew to your vessel." Lukas glanced her with an eyebrow rather than verbalizing 'stupid.'

"The damage can't be that bad Griffin." Sahra seemed hesitant.

"In danger of ripping the whole port out. I'll see what my engineers can do, give me twenty minutes."

"Oh you must think me stupid, fix that and you'll be out of here. No, you turn Argo around now." Sahra's usual charm brightened everyone's day.

"I couldn't get out of here before you blew us into scrap metal and spaghetti sauce Lieutenant."

"Very well," Sahra huffed "evacuate the women, if anyone attempts to disembark shuttles they will be shot. Is that clear? You dock and stay put."

"Crystal. Prepare to receive shortly." Lukas cut communications.

"Captain!?" Yoto couldn't believe they'd given up so easily.

"Marines?"

"No, Lieutenant Sahra Panty Bunch is obviously out of her depth. Both Saber and Leviathan probably have skeleton crews. If a Lieutenant is the most experienced officer they can send against us, I would imagine the fleet has troubles elsewhere. So they won't

have any interceptor or hawk pilots. Two Eagles, but we have the fighters. What's their bearing Kartha?"
"Port and starboard Captain. Giving us a warm hug no doubt."
"Stupid woman, shuttles can make it back to Lunar Station all by them little selves." Mike commented.
"No, you have to understand the mind of a rising anal officer, she wants the glory and butt kissing of handing over the prize herself. Within a week this surrender would become an epic battle won by her heroic self and... well you get the picture."

Lukas briefed pilots on tactics. Grant, naming the new shuttle Phantom, took her out slowly, while Jorgen readied Huntress to launch. Saber's bay doors opened to receive shuttles, like a mouth waiting for an evil dentist to inflict pain.

"What's your pilot playing at Griffin?" Sahra became irritated at Phantom's dithering.
"One moment Lieutenant, our damage is stabilized, we can return to Lunar Station now if you would prefer." Lukas avoided temptation of theatrical begging or using terms like 'Your Highness'.
"Very well." Sahra's eyes rolled "Get on with it."
"Take her under Ensign." Lukas nonchalantly commanded for the Argo to turn about, taking her under Saber.
"Under... way Captain." Kartha confirmed.
"And take it real slow Griffin." Sahra waved for the Saber to turn and escort.
"See you in Hell Lieutenant." Lukas gave his own command wave; resulting in auxiliary weapons ripping a new hole in Saber's launch bay.

Ravens shot from launch tubes like bullets, barely clearing the hull before extending combat wings, they arced around; sights set on Leviathan. Huntress roared from Argo's launch bay, while Grant activated Phantom's combat status. Auxiliary cannons continued to fire; blasting away at Saber's underside as Argo crept beneath. Behind her; multiple minor explosions indicated ravens hitting their mark; Leviathan's main port cannons disintegrating under a relentless assault of blue laser fire, exploding as interceptors raced over and under her. Grant and Jorgen brought hawks around unleashing fury at Leviathan's engine ports, thundering over exploding auxiliary cannons amidst numerous hull impacts; shaking Leviathan's superstructure. Saber tried to turn, her auxiliary cannons firing at raven's and hawks; only managing a glancing blow at Huntress's wing. Leviathan's starboard cannons fired before raven's could disarms them, Phantom reeled under the critical strike, spinning out of control, generators exploding, flames spewing from her fuselage.

"Grant, eject, eject." Lukas barely had a second to spare the pilot before a raven exploded above Saber; killing Rodrigo.

Leviathan listed, her engines and guns twisted wreckage. Huntress arced through a fireball that was once Phantom, in a slow spin Jorgen vented on Leviathan's bow. Saber's starboard and auxiliary cannons wrecked, Argo reversed thrusters, slipping out from under her, bringing main pulse cannons to bare, Argo fired once destroying Saber's engine ports.

"You have ten minutes to evacuate Lieutenant Garson, before I finish the job." Lukas sat back.
"Picking up Grant Sir, he seems okay." Jorgen notified.
"Good, otherwise I'd have to kick his dead butt." Lukas breathed a sigh of relief.
"You won't get far Griffin, half the fleet is preparing to launch." Sahra spat.
"I thought you were half the fleet Sahra, you're ass is big enough. Where's everyone anyway? Oh you have nine minutes to get your butt out of there."
"Very well." Sahra jabbed a wave at whoever else was on Saber's Bridge, before ending communications.
"Get those birds back, and let's be on our way before they send anything else."
"Yes Sir, two ravens docked already." Yoto reported.
"Captain, multiple bandits bearing one six five point two four, ETA twenty minutes." Kartha tried to determine numbers and class of ships.
"They won't find anything but wreckage, I'm not leaving these

eagles to haunt us." Lukas brought up tactical on his display.

With the battle storm subsiding, Caron returned to check on Arten and Yun, inviting them to join her and others in the mess hall as they were all hungry. Despite initial reluctance from one who had no need of food, Caron mentioning that Dharma was joining them persuaded Arten to accompany Yun, although he didn't want to deal with fear or hostility from those that had seen his other state. Arten's spirits raised to cheering and thanks from what few crew members occupied the mess hall and virtually everyone on the way there. He'd become the darling and savior of every mother aboard.

"Ahhh, see not such a monster after all eh!" Jack attacked a cheeseburger.
"No mow glumpy face." Yun squeezed Arten's knee, while trying to tempt him with a French fry.
"You need to speak propa English like wot I does." Caron smirked.
"I speaky jus fine." Yun poked her tongue out.

"Their hawks are attacking, direct hits to starboard and stern Sir." Kartha yelled.
"Fire. Evasive. Jorgen kill that Bitch." Lukas needn't ask; Jorgen let rip on one hawk, Argo's auxiliary cannons began to shred the second, as Argo turned to face the assault.
"Coming in too fast sir, brace for…" Kartha tensed expectantly.

Argo screamed under impact of an exploding hawk, disintegrating over her upper hull, fuselage smashing auxiliary cannons, flaming debris catapulting steps of thunder and screeching metal, while what remained of the hawk's hull screamed against the Argo, rotating before finally exploding over engine ports. Argo lurched forward, thrown into a horizontal slow spin out before Saber's bow and one remaining port cannon, which fired, narrowly missing Argo, whose spin now brought her cannons to bare.

"FIRE!" Lukas briefly saw the image of Sahra smirking, still on Saber's Bridge, before air became fire as Saber vented blooms from ruptured fuselage, Argo's cannon's recoiled again and again sending electric blue fury into a growing inferno, listing toward

Leviathan. "Full reverse thrusters, launch missiles."
"Yes Sir, that's about all we have left, engine ports are totaled." Heather shook her head at a growing number of alerts. "Hera, critical damage report."
"Engines inoperable. Auxiliary weapons destroyed. Superficial damage to hull, integrity one hundred percent."
"We're safe, but a sitting duck. What's the ETA on that fleet?" Lukas slammed a hand down on his chair's arm.
"Eleven minutes to optimal range Sir." Kartha turned around to face Lukas as if to say 'what do we do now?'
"Crap." Lukas held on as what remained of Saber collided with Leviathan; resulting in a huge explosion, blasting Argo toward the sun, throwing debris at her for good measure. "Geeshh that was close." he watched two massive chunks of fuselage vaporized by Argo's cannons before they impacted. "Jorgen, Grant report."
"Taken a bashing Captain, coming in." Jorgen tried to hold a vibrating Huntress steady.
"Make it quick, we need to launch remaining hawks to tow us outta here." Lukas knew there was little hope for them now without propulsion, but anything was better than drifting into the sun's inferno.
"Entering launch bay now Sir." Jorgen retracted wings as the shuttle approached lights of the landing bay. "Instruments giving strange readings Captain."

"I don't feel right." Dharma still lay on the mess hall floor, while others picked themselves up.
"What's up?" Caron walked on all fours to her side.
"I don't know, scared, I don't." Dharma felt fear, not so much her own, beyond her or crew and yet for everyone. "I don't feel right." Holding her abdomen, tears streamed from eyes as images of unborn babies filled Dharma's mind.
"Monique, Clair, anyone mess hall emergency." Caron almost screamed into her suit's communicator; fearing the worst. "Hang in there Dharma."
"What's the problem?" Monique rushed toward the mess hall.
"I think there... just get here quick." Caron didn't want to alarm Dharma further.
"Hey can't you use your healing?" Arten knelt by his Sister.

"Noo Aahgh." Dharma sat up, bent over in pain.
"Just hold on girl." Caron held Dharma, trying to hold back her own tears.

"Sensors going crazy Sir" Heather stared at instruments showing meters rising and falling, alarm warnings activating, deactivating.
"Same here Captain." Kartha reported "Loosing all controls."
"Shit, damn Science Division must have come up with some kind of disrupter." Mike concluded.
"Jorgen, are your systems malfunctioning? Jorgen… Dammit no communication. Hera report." Lukas, slouched, resigning himself to the inevitable.
"Wow, weird shit." Heather stepped back from her console that briefly warped with colors.

"Let me have a look at you, lay down for me." Monique tried to ease Dharma back.
"AOooowww, nah no, it burns." Dharma could barely define anything other than pain, fear and indescribable images racing through her mind, she had only seen them once before "Ohh." Her eyes seemed to glaze, contradicting a moment of mental clarity.
"Can I have some room here." Monique waved at the crowd of concerned crew. "Dharma, no lay down please." She became alarmed as Dharma stood up, spreading her arms out to either side.
"Dharma?"
"Oh God!" Jack fell to his knees gazing up at Dharma's black eyes speckled with stars.
"Don't look, don't look." Caron remembered what Thoth had warned, wrenching her own eyes away and pounced on Jack.

Everyone was looking, staring at walls, tables, a floor that rippled with colors, Argo's structure seemed to ripple becoming translucent. Dharma's mouth gaped open wide, from it issued a song, a melody, a note of no language known to any mortal, so utterly beautiful, crew members almost passed out; enchanted, captivated as if every cell of their being wanted to dance and shine. Arten gazed down at his legs, like everything else their form became indistinct, rippling, awash with a spectrum of colors. Everything and everyone began to merge into one until Dharma song ended. In that instant came a sense of being sucked into a black hole, then nothing but a tiny point of white light, a sparkle in Dharma's eye.

She blinked.

"Are we nearly there yet?" Lukas still covered his eyes with hands.
"Uhh…. I think so." Kartha scrutinized navigational instruments.
"Any…"
"Yes hundreds of giant space frogs, we're surrounded. Battle stations, arm the fly swat!"
"Hey I give the orders around here Mike! Belay that fly swat. Okay so where are we? I'll save the how for later." Lukas tried to focus eyes on a red dot above a hazy bluish white crescent.
"Orbiting, err, I don't know. Six planets in a red dwarf system." Heather tried to reorganize her brain cells, which didn't quite seem to be where they should. "Did you hear that music?"
"Yes, it was so… I don't know." Yoto scratched his head.
"Hera, where are we?" Lukas felt the same indescribable way, but focused on more pressing matters.
"Unknown Lukas."
"Ohh, Lukas is it now, hands off Hera he's mine." Kartha's eyebrows raised.
"Oh he's not my type." Hera's increasing seductive tone and terminology brought with it more mystery.
"What!?" Lukas didn't know whether to laugh or scream at Hera's very incomputerate personality. "Err what is your type Hera?"'
"Well you'll have to build him for me darling." Hera would smile if she had a face.
"Ooohhhhkay, I'll add that to my to-do list." Lukas glared, wide eyed.
"Don't you just love Thoth's sense of humor!" Mike grinned.
"I'd rather he were here cracking jokes, at least he could tell us where the heck we are." Lukas, sat bewildered.
"Orbiting a planet with oceans, continents and life. Stable tectonic plates and… pyramids." Heather informed.
"Oh, here we go again. At least we're alive."
"Yes but in a decaying orbit Captain." Kartha warned.
"Let's use what we have and take a look." Lukas gestured to the

screen.

"There's some kind of beacon, no idea if the signal is saying anything, just transmitting a single tone." Heather turned to the Captain.

"Can we land near it Kartha?"

"It's located at a large coastal bay, but Argo's in bad shape Sir, be lucky to land anywhere!"

"Take her in over the ocean, use magnetic landing polarity to hold us up if possible." Lukas commanded before opening a com channel to the crew. "Brace for impact, emergency landing." He alerted, causing a flurry of activity and helmet activations.

Argo's decent velocity increased rapidly, thrusters screaming to avoid disaster as they fell toward a blue violet ocean, calm, serene, ripples gently waved under influence of a single moon, presently hiding from the sun. A moment of thunder disrupted tranquility, before the ocean bloomed as Argo impacted, sending high waves racing across its surface a traumatized watery domain. Argo descended into darkness, smashing into the ocean floor before rising again. She skidded, impacting rock, sand and reef leaving a trail of chaos. Magnetic repelling finally stabilized Argo's flight, now slowing she raised to the surface, water streaming from her hull that glittered sunlight.

"Thank you for traveling with Argo Spaceways!" Lukas picked himself off the floor once again "We hope you had a pleasant trip!"

"You want an answer to that?" Mike groaned.

"No."

"The beacon is just over two thousand clicks from here." Heather informed, deactivating her helmet. "Thrusters…. Still operable."

"Be there in a few minutes Sir." Kartha engaged.

Argo gracefully glided into the bay, until magnetic landing buffers eased her down onto huge landing stanchions, that's claws sunk beneath sand. Argo hissed the hull down as if breathing a sign of relief, while crew assembled at main disembarkation hatches waiting for a recon team to report.

"Yeah air's safe, initial readings say were on Ashari to cut a long

story short Captain." Anwar reported.
"Okay, let's get some sunshine people, just be cautious, don't stray far from the ship."
"It is just like Ashari." Mike commented stepping onto sand, gazing around at distant vegetation, a lavender tint to ocean waves and orange glow in the sky.
"Let's check out that beacon." Caron strided across the beach, dragging Jack behind by his wrist.
"HELP, I'm being abducted by Spiderwoman!" Jack laughed.
"Come on." Caron waved to others.

Sand became dune and then grass before Caron squatted by a two foot high obelisk with no distinguishing marks jutting out of sandy soil. Jack, the twins, Mike, Lukas, Kartha and Yun stood around waiting in vain for Caron to reveal some fascinating information.

"No known material, same signal." Mike shrugged.
"Must be teaming with life here," Lukas gazed around guardedly watching nearby forestation.
"It's just like home." Dharma smiled broadly.
"Well you brought us here girl." Jack commented.
"Guess she was homesick." Arten squeezed her hand "At least you're okay now."
"Can't see anything on it." Caron's hands brushed over the black obelisk "Feels cold… oh, ooohhh dear!" She stood back, as did others watching the obelisk rise higher and higher.
"You gone an done it now woman, what did I tell you about touching big pointy things!" Jack grabbed Caron's hand, stepping further back as a mound of sand and soil piled higher around the obelisk's base.
"Ya got me in enough trouble as it is!" Caron shielded her eyes gazing up at the ninety feet high monument.
"Look there's three more." Arten pointed out three smaller obelisks risen from the ground to the East, South and West
"Probably one in the North as well in that forest.
"Yeah, definitely movement. Anwar, take your squad and check North of my position. Maybe we should remove our little selves before something blows up or starts shooting at us." Lukas suggested.

"No, no wait look." Caron pointed at a long shadow caste by the main obelisk. "It's like a huge sundial."

"What is this?" Dharma, squatting; examining one image engraved on all four sides of the obelisk.

"It's an old device used to measure time, Dharma. An hourglass." Caron knelt beside her.

"Then I guess humanity better get it right this time." Lukas's eyes met those around him.

"Sir, we have, errr, company… I think." Anwar didn't quite know what to report as he stood next to Mahindra in the forest.

"You think?" Lukas was in no mood for more unpleasant surprises.

"Well…. Mahindra is talking to a carrot…. I think." Anwar shook his head, not understanding carrot sign language.

"Is it armed?" Lukas tried to keep a straight face.

"No, just leafed!"

An invisible presence observed, content to let things be for now. There were other worlds to create, other souls waiting to become… something.

THE BEGINNING

About the author

Phoenix Mackenzie is no stranger to the strange, the mysterious and esoteric (hidden knowledge). To him what dwells beyond dimensional veils is his world. Whether that is fiction or fact is left for you to discover as now after many years of writing, his stories are gradually being shared with the unsuspecting public.

Gravity Wave was written before the catastrophe in Japan, freak weather patterns in Australia, America and elsewhere. Before the uprising against governments in the Middle East, what was fiction is now becoming fact.

Forthcoming publications:

Shadow Makers (Science Fiction.)
Gravity Wave continues. After forty years of peace darkness descends upon the distant colony of Nirvani, having first reaped a human harvest from Earth. Argo must spread her wings once again, yet Earth lies 80,000 light years distant at our galaxies far side and the forces she must face are formidable. Is there any hope? Something steps from the shadows and whispers 'Maybe'.

Mythic Keys (Fantasy.)
What creature are you? A vampire, ogre, elf, dragon or one of the many others figments of imagination, what is your nature, what lurks within? A fool meddling in dark arts and alcohol discovers that this is not the only dimension in which life and death dance together. The lords of existence insure that such realms mind their own business until Lord Crow breaks all the rules, becoming the hapless victim of a myth realm and subjecting humanity to a similar fate. Will an ancient elemental wizard set things right, or will he just observe; amused by the chaos that ensues? Well if you had been bored for two hundred thousand years what would you do!

CPSIA information can be obtained at www.ICGtesting.com
Printed in the USA
266475BV00001B/9/P